ESPRIT DE CORPS
and
STIFF UPPER LIP

D1158855

by Lawrence Durrell

JUSTINE

BALTHAZAR

MOUNTOLIVE

CLEA

THE BLACK BOOK

BITTER LEMONS

ESPRIT DE CORPS

STIFF UPPER LIP

SAPPHO

COLLECTED POEMS

PROSPERO'S CELL *and* REFLECTIONS
    ON A MARINE VENUS

POPE JOAN

THE DARK LABYRINTH

ESPRIT DE CORPS
and
STIFF UPPER LIP

by

LAWRENCE DURRELL

Illustrated by

VASILIU

and

NICOLAS BENTLEY

A Dutton  *Paperback*

NEW YORK

E. P. DUTTON & CO., INC.

This paperback edition of
"ESPRIT DE CORPS"
and
"STIFF UPPER LIP"
Published 1961 by E. P. Dutton & Co., Inc.
All rights reserved. Printed in the U.S.A.
"ESPRIT DE CORPS"
Copyright, ©, 1957, by Lawrence Durrell
"STIFF UPPER LIP"
Copyright, ©, 1958, 1959, by Lawrence George Durrell

No part of this book may be reproduced in any form whatsoever without permission in writing from the publisher, except by a reviewer who wishes to quote brief passages in connection with a review written for inclusion in a magazine or newspaper or broadcasts.

Inscribed to the members of the Chancery,
H.M. Embassy Belgrade 1951.

LAWRENCE DURRELL, a British citizen of Irish parentage, was born in the Himalaya region of India. His first ten years were spent in India. After schooling in England, he decided to become a writer. Throughout the 1930's Mr. Durrell devoted most of his talents to his poetry which has won much acclaim. His first novel, *The Black Book*, was published in Paris in 1938, and was cited by T. S. Eliot as being one of the great hopes for modern English fiction. *The Black Book* was published in the United States for the first time in 1960.

World War II temporarily interrupted Mr. Durrell's literary career. During the war years and for some time thereafter, he served Great Britain in various official and diplomatic capacities in Athens, Cairo, Rhodes and Belgrade.

The publication of *Justine* in 1957, and the subsequent appearance of *Balthazar* (1958), *Mountolive* (1959), and *Clea* (1960) as parts of the same magnificent series called "The Alexandria Quartet" devoted to an examination of the various aspects of love, immediately caused Mr. Durrell to be recognized as one of the greatest and most important writers of modern times.

ESPRIT DE CORPS was first published in 1958; STIFF UPPER LIP first appeared in 1959.

Esprit de Corps

Contents

The Ghost Train

I like Antrobus. I can't really say why—I think it is because he takes everything so frightfully seriously. He is portentous—always dropping into a whisper, clicking his tongue, making a po-face, pursing his lips, turning the palms of his hand outwards and making "what-would-you" gestures.

We've served together in a number of foreign capitals, he as a regular of the career, I as a contract officer: which explains why he is now a heavily padded senior in Southern while I am an impoverished writer. Nevertheless, whenever I'm in London he gives me lunch at his club and we talk about the past—those happy days passed in foreign capitals "lying abroad" for our country.

"The Ghost Train episode", said Antrobus, "was a bit before your time. I only mention it because I can think of nothing which illustrates the peculiar hazards of Diplomatic Life so well. In fact it throws them into Stark Relief.

"Every nation has its particular *idée fixe*. For the Yugoslavs it is trains. Nothing can compare for breathtaking romance with the railway train. Railway engines have to be put under armed guard when not in motion or they would be poked to pieces by the enquiring peasantry. No other object arouses the concupiscence of the Serb like a train. They drool over it, old boy, positively drool. *Ils bavent*.

"You twig this the minute you alight from the Orient Express at Belgrade because there is something queer about the station building itself. It leans to one side. It is neatly cracked from platform level to clock-tower. Moreover there are several distinct sets of ruts in the concrete of the platform which are highly suggestive. The first porter you engage will clear up the mystery. Apparently every fifteenth train or so leaps the buffers, grinds across the Freight Section and buries itself in the booking office. No one is ever hurt and the whole town joyfully bands together to dig the engine out. Everyone is rather proud of this particular idiosyncrasy. It is part of the Serbian way of life.

"Well, being aware of this as I was, I could not help being a bit concerned when Nimic in the Protocol hinted that the Diplomatic Corps was to be sent to Zagreb for Liberation Day in a special train which would prove once and for all that the much-vaunted Yugoslav heavy industry was capable of producing machinery every bit as good as the degenerate Capitalist West. This tip was accompanied by dark looks and winks and all efforts to probe the mystery further proved vain. A veil of secrecy (one of the seven veils of Communist diplomacy) was drawn over the subject. Naturally we in the Corps were interested, while those who had served for some time in the Balkans were perturbed. '*Mon Dieu*,' said Du Bellay the

Vasiliu

French Minister gravely, '*si ces animaux veulent jouer aux locos avec le Corps Diplomatique . . .*' He was voicing the Unspoken Thoughts of many of us.

"There was no further information forthcoming about the Ghost Train as we jokingly called it, so we sat back and waited for Liberation Day. Sure enough the customary fat white envelope appeared ten days before from the Protocol. I opened mine with a troubled curiosity. It announced that the Corps would be travelling by a Special Train which would be placed at its disposal. The train itself was called 'The Liberation-Celebration Machine'.

"Even Polk-Mowbray looked a bit grave. 'What sort of Devil-Car do you think it will be?' he said apprehensively. I couldn't enlighten him, alas. 'It's probably a chain-drive Trojan with some carriages built around it in plywood.'

"There was a short-lived movement among the Corps to go by road instead and thus sidestep the 'Liberation-Celebration Machine' but the Doyen put his foot down. Such a defection would constitute a grave slight. The Yugoslav heavy industry would be hurt by our refusal to allow it to unveil the marvels of modern science to us. Reluctantly we all accepted. 'Butch' Benbow, the naval attaché, who was clairvoyant and who dabbled in astrology, took the omens. Apparently they were not propitious. 'All I can see is clouds of smoke,' he said hoarsely, looking up from the progressed chart on his desk. 'And someone gets a severe scalp wound—probably you, sir.'

"Polk-Mowbray started. 'Now, look here,' he said, 'let's have no alarm and despondency on this one. If the Yugoslav heavy industry gives me even a trifling scalp wound I'll see that there is an International Incident over it.'

"The day drew inexorably nearer. The Special Train, we learned, was to be met in a siding just outside Belgrade. There is a small station there, the name of which I forget. Here at the appointed time, which was dusk, we duly presented ourselves in full *tenue*. There were to be flowers and speeches by representatives of the Yugoslav Heavy Industry. Most of the representatives looked nearly as heavy as their industry. But I couldn't take my eyes off the train.

"I'm not saying it was gaudy. It was absolutely breathtaking. The three long coaches were made of painted and carved timber; flowers, birds, liberation heroes, *cachesexes*, emblematic devices, post-horns—everything you can imagine, all carved and painted according to the peasant fancy. The general effect was that of a Sicilian market-cart with painted and carved side-boards—or the poop of some seventeenth-century galleon. Every blacksmith, wheelwright and cartwright in Serbia must have had a hand in it. '*C'est un chalet Tyroléan ou quoi?*' I heard Du Bellay say under his breath. His scepticism was shared by us all.

"We entered and found our reserved carriages which seemed normal enough. The band played. We accepted a wreath or two. Then we set off in the darkness to the braying of donkeys and cocks and the rasping of trombones. We were off across the rolling Serbian plains.

"Two things were immediately obvious. All this elaborate woodwork squeaked and groaned calamitously, ear-splittingly. How were we to get any sleep? But more serious still was the angle of inclination of the second coach with the Heads of Mission in it. It was about thirty degrees out of centre and was only, it seemed, held up-right by the one immediately before and behind it. It was clear that the Yugoslav heavy industry had mislaid its spirit-level while it was under construction. People who looked out of the windows on one side had the illusion that the ground was coming up to hit them. I paid Polk-Mowbray a visit to see if he was all right and found him looking rather pale, and drawn up on the higher elevation of the coach like someone on a sinking ship. The noise was so great that we couldn't speak—we had to shout: 'My God,' I heard him cry out, 'what is to become of us all?' It was a little difficult to say. We were now gathering speed. The engine was a very old one. It had been abandoned before the war by an American film company and the Yugoslavs had tied it together with wire. Its gaping furnace, which was white hot, was being passion-ately fed by some very hairy men in cloth caps who looked like Dostoevsky's publishers. It seemed to me that the situation had never looked graver. Despite its age, however, it had managed to whip up a good forty-five. And every five hundred yards it would groan and void a bucketful of white clinker into the night which set fire to the grass on either side of the track. From far off we must have looked like an approaching forest fire.

"Another feature of the 'Liberation-Celebration Machine' was an ingenious form of central heating which could not be turned off, and as none of the windows opened, the temperature inside the coaches rapidly mounted into the hundreds. People were fanning them-selves with their tall hats. Old man, never have I seen the Corps subjected to such a strain. Sleep was impossible. The lights would not turn off. The wash basins appeared to empty into each other. And all the time we had the ghastly thought of all the Heads of Mission in the Hanging Coach, drinking brandy and gibbering with fright as we sped onwards through the night.

"The chance of some frightful accident taking place was far from remote and consequently nobody was able to relax. We did not even dare to get into pyjamas but sat about in that infernal racket staring desperately at one another and starting at every regurgitation of the engine, every shiver and squeak of the coaches. The American Ambassador was so overcome that he spent the night singing 'Nearer My God To Thee'. Some said that he had had the forethought to take a case of rye into his compartment with him. Madame Fawzia, the Egyptian Ambassadress, spent the night on the floor of her compartment deep in prayer. I simply did not dare to think of Polk-Mowbray. From time to time when the wind changed the whole train was enveloped in a cloud of rich dense smoke containing fragments of half-digested coal the size of hailstones. But still the ghoulish crew in the engine-cab plied their grisly shovels and on we sped with mournful shrieks and belches.

"At two in the morning there was a ghastly rending noise as we entered the station of Slopsy Blob, named after the famous Independence fighter. The Hanging Coach somehow got itself engaged with the tin dado which ran along the roof of the station and ripped it off as clean as a whistle, by the same token almost decapitating one of the drivers. The noise was appalling and the whole Corps let out a unified shriek of terror. I have never heard diplomats scream like that before or since—and I never want to. A lot of cherubs and floral devices were ripped off the Hanging Coach in the encounter and the people in the rear coaches found themselves assailed by a hail of coloured fragments of wood which made them shriek the louder. It was all over in a moment.

"Then we were out in the night once more racing across the dark plain, the brothers Karamazov still plying the engine with might and main. It is possible that, in the manner of Serbs, they had heard nothing. We spent the rest of the night in Sleepless Vigil, old man. The guardian angel of the Yugoslav Heavy Industry must have been with us for nothing much worse happened. But it was a pretty dispirited and shaken dip corps that was finally dragged into Zagreb station on that Liberation morning. I can tell you, never was liberation so much in the forefront of everyone's thoughts.

"It must have been about six o'clock when we stormed into Zagreb squealing and blowing out an Etna of steam. The brakes had been applied some three miles outside the station and their ear-splitting racket had to be heard to be believed.

"But this was not the end. Though we missed the red carpet by a quarter of a mile, and though the waiting dignitaries and the Zagreb Traction and Haulage Workers' Band padded down the platform after us our troubles were not yet at an end. It was found that the doors of the coaches on the platform side were fast shut and could not be opened. I suppose Zagreb Station must have been on the opposite side of the track from Belgrade Station and consequently nobody dreamed that we should need more than one exit from the train. It was, of course, fearfully humiliating. We leaned against the windows making inarticulate gestures of goodwill and vague grimaces in the direction of the Traction Haulage Workers' Band and the Liberation Reception Committee.

"We must have looked like a colony of dispossessed fairground apes pining for the old life of the trees. After a good deal of mopping and mowing there was nothing for it but to climb out of the Zagreb Flyer on to the permanent way and walk round the train to the reception point. This we somewhat shamefacedly did. But when all was said and done it was good to feel terra firma under our feet once more. Drawn up in order of precedence on Zagreb platform we submitted to the Liberation anthem sung by the Partisan choir in a register so low that it could not drown the merry cries of self-congratulation with which the Karamazov brothers were greeting the morn. Their observations were punctuated by blasts of hot steam and whiffs of sound from the whistle of the Liberation-Celebration Machine which looked even more improbable in the cold morning light than it had done the evening before.

"All this went off as well as such things can be expected to do; but sleepy as we were a sudden chill struck our hearts at a phrase in the Speech of Welcome which plainly indicated that the authorities were expecting us to make the return journey in the Liberation-Celebration Machine on the following day. This gave us all food for thought. Madame Fawzia made an involuntary retching noise which was interpreted by our hosts as an expression of joy. Several other ladies in the Corps showed a disposition to succumb to the vapours at this piece of intelligence. But the old training dies hard. There was many a tight lip and beady eye but not a word was said until we were assembled for breakfast in the card room of the Slopsy Blob Hotel. Then the pent-up floodwaters of emotion overflowed. Ambassadors, Ministers, Secretaries of Embassy and their wives began as one man to gesticulate and gabble. It was a moving scene. Some called upon the Gods to witness that they would never travel by train again; others spoke wonderingly of the night they had just spent when the whole of their past life flashed before them as if on a screen; the wife of the Spanish Republican Minister, by far the most deeply shaken by events, fell upon the Doyen, the Polish Ambassador, and named him as responsible before God for our safety and well-being. It was an interesting study in national types. The Egyptians screamed, the Finns and Norwegians snarled, the Slav belt pulled at each other's lapels as if they were milking goats. The Greeks made Promethean gestures at everyone. (They could afford to take the Balanced View since they had already hired the only six taxis in Zagreb and were offering seats for the return journey at a thousand dinars each.)

"One thing emerged clearly from all this. The Corps was in a state of open mutiny and would not easily be persuaded to entrain once more with the Brothers Karamazov. The Doyen pleaded in vain. We struck various national attitudes all round the room. The Italian Ambassadress who looked as if her anger would succeed in volatilizing her went so far as to draw up her dress and show the company a bruise inflicted on her during the journey. As for Polk-Mowbray, he did indeed have a scalp wound—an egg-shaped protuberance on the crown of his head where he had doubtless been struck by a passing railway station. It was clear that the journey had aged him.

"Well, that day most of us spent the time in bed with cold compresses and aspirin. In the evening we attended a performance of the Ballet and a Torchlight Tattoo. Liberation Day was at an end. That night the Doyen convened another meeting in the hotel at which he harangued us about diplomatic procedure in general and our obligations to the Service in particular. In vain. We were determined not to travel back on the Ghost Train. He pleaded with us but we were adamant. That evening a flock of telegrams fluttered into the Protocol Department of the Ministry of Foreign Affairs—telegrams pleading sudden illness, pressure of work, unforeseen political developments, migraine, influenza, neuritis or Events Beyond the Writer's Control. At dawn a convoy of taxis set out on the homeward track bearing the shattered remnants of the Corps, unshaven, unhonoured, but still alive, still breathing. . . . In a way I was sorry for the Brothers Karamazov and the Liberation-Celebration Machine. God knows, one did not wish them ill. But I must confess I was not surprised to read in the paper a week later that this latest triumph of the Yugoslav Heavy Industry had jumped the points at Slopsy Blob and finished the good work it had begun by carrying away most of the station buildings. No one was hurt. No one ever is in Serbia. Just badly shaken and frightened out of one's wits. It is all, when you come to think of it, part of the Serbian Way of Life. . . ."

Case History

Last week, Polk-Mowbray's name came up again—we had read of his retirement that morning, in *The Times*. We had both served under him in Madrid and Moscow, while Antrobus himself had been on several missions headed by him—Sir Claud Polk-Mowbray, O.M., K.C.M.G., and all that sort of thing.

Talking of him, Antrobus did his usual set of facial jerks culminating in an expression like a leaky flowerpot, and said: "You know, old man, thinking of Polk-Mowbray today and all the different places we've served, I suddenly thought 'My God, in Polk-Mowbray we have witnessed the gradual destruction of an Ambassador's soul'."

I was startled by this observation.

"I mean," went on Antrobus, "that gradually, insidiously, the Americans got him."

"How do you mean, 'the Americans got him'?"

Antrobus clicked his tongue and lofted his gaze.

"Perhaps you didn't know, perhaps you were not a Silent Witness as I was."

CASE HISTORY

"I don't honestly think I was."

"Do you remember Athens '37, when I was first secretary?"

"Of course."

"Polk-Mowbray was a perfectly normal well-balanced Englishman then. He had all the fashionable weaknesses of the eighteenth-century gentleman. He fenced, he played the recorder."

"I remember all that."

"But something else too. Think back."

"I'm thinking. . . ."

Antrobus leaned forward and said with portentous triumph: "He wrote good English in those days." Then he sat back and stared impressively at me down the long bony incline of his nose. He allowed the idea to soak in.

Of course what he meant by good English was the vaguely orotund and ornamental eighteenth-century stuff which was then so much in vogue. A sort of mental copperplate prose.

"I remember now," I said, "committing the terrible sin of using the phrase 'the present set-up' in a draft despatch on economics." (It came back gashed right through with the scarlet pencil which only Governors and Ambassadors are allowed to wield—and with something nasty written in the margin.)

"Ah," said Antrobus, "so you remember that. What did he write?"

" 'The thought that members of my staff are beginning to introject American forms into the Mother Tongue has given me great pain. I am ordering Head of Chancery to instruct staff that no despatches to the Foreign Secretary should contain phrases of this nature.' "

"Phew."

"As you say—phew."

"But Nemesis", said Antrobus, "was lying in wait for him, old chap. Mind you," he added in the sort of tone which always sounds massively hypocritical to foreigners simply because it is, "mind you I'm not anti-American myself—never was, never will be. And there were some things about the old Foreign Office Prose Style—the early Nicolson type."

"It was practically Middle English."

"No, what I objected to was the Latin tag. Polk-Mowbray was always working one in. If possible he liked to slip one in at the beginning of a despatch. '*Hominibus plenum, amicis vacuum* as Cato says', he would kick off. The damnable thing was that at times he would forget whether it was Cato who said it. I was supposed to know, as Head of Chancery. But I never did. My classics have always been fluffy. I used to flash to my Pears Encyclopedia or my Brewer, swearing all the time."

"He sacked young Pollit for attributing a remark in Tacitus to Suetonius."

"Yes. It was very alarming. I'm glad those days are over."

"But Nemesis. What form did he take?"

"She, old man. *She*. Nemesis is always a woman. Polk-Mowbray was sent on a brief mission to the States in the middle of the war."

"Ah."

"He saw her leading a parade wrapped in the Stars and Stripes and twirling a baton. Her name was Carrie Potts. She was what is known as a majorette. I know. Don't wince. No, he didn't marry her. But she was a Milestone, old fellow. From then on the change came about, very

gradually, very insidiously. I noticed that he dropped the
Latin tag in his drafts. Then he began to leave the 'u' out
of words like 'colour' and 'valour'. Finally, and this is
highly significant, he sent out a staff circular saying that
any of the secretaries caught using phrases like *quid pro
quo*, *sine qua non*, *ad hoc*, *ab initio*, *ab ovo* and *status quo* would
be transferred. This was a bombshell. We were deprived
at a blow of practically our whole official vocabulary.
Moreover as he read through the circular I distinctly
heard him say under his breath: 'This will pin their ears
back.' You can imagine, old fellow, I was stiff with horror. Of course, the poor fellow is not entirely to blame;
he was fighting the disease gamely enough. It was just
too much for him. I found a book by Damon Runyon in
his desk-drawer one day. I admit that he had the good
taste to blush when he saw I'd found it. But by this time
he had begun to suffer from dreadful slips of the tongue.
At a cocktail party for instance he referred to me as his
'sidekick'. I was too polite to protest but I must admit it
rankled. But there was a much more serious aspect to the
business. His despatches began to take a marked trans-
pontine turn. By God, you'll never believe it but I kept
coming across expressions like 'set-up', 'frame-up',
'come-back', and even 'gimmick'. I ask you—*gimmick*."
Antrobus blew out his breath in a cloud of horror. "As
you can imagine," he went on after a pause, "the F.O.
was troubled by the change in his reporting. Worst of all,
other Ministers and Ambassadors junior to him and easily
influenced showed some disposition to copy this sort of
thing. Finally it got to such a pitch that all despatches
before being printed in Intel-summary form had to pass
through a sieve: they established an office in the Rehabili-
tation section specially for deformed English. Then you

remember the Commission on Official English and the book called *Foreign Office Prose—How to Write It*?"

"Yes. One of the worst written books I've ever read."

"Well, be that as it may, it was the direct outcome of Polk-Mowbray's activities. It was a last desperate attempt to stop the rot, old man. It was too late, of course, because by this time that dreadful Churchill chap was wandering all over the globe in a siren suit waving a Juliet at everyone. I need hardly add that Mowbray himself ordered a siren suit which he referred to as his 'sneakers'. He used to potter round the Embassy grounds in them— a bit furtively, of course, but nevertheless . . . there it was." Antrobus paused for a long moment as he sorted out these painful memories. Then he said grimly, under his breath, and with dark contempt: "Faucet, elevator, phoney. I *ask* you."

"Yes," I said.

"Hatchet-man . . . disc-jockey . . . torch-singer."

"Yes. Yes. I follow you."

"I was terribly sad. Poor Polk-Mowbray. Do you know that he went to a Rotary meeting in a hand-painted tie depicting a nude blonde and referred to it in his speech as 'pulchritudinous'?"

"Never."

"He did." Antrobus nodded vigorously several times and took a savage swig at his drink. "He absolutely did."

"I suppose", I said after a moment, "that now he is retiring he will settle over there and integrate himself."

"He was offered a chance to go to Lake Success as a specialist on Global Imponderables, but he turned it down. Said the I.Q. wasn't high enough—whatever that meant. No, it's even more tragic. He has taken a villa outside Rome and intends to summer in Italy. I saw him

24

Vasiliu

last week when I came back from the Athens Conference."

"You saw him?"

"Yes." Antrobus fell into a heavy brooding silence, evidently stirred to the quick. "I don't really know if I should tell you this," he said in a voice with a suspicion of choking in it. "It's such a nightmare."

"I won't repeat it."

"No. Please don't."

"I won't."

He gazed sadly at me as he signed his bar slips, waiting in true Foreign Office style until the servant was out of earshot. Then he leaned forward and said: "I ran into him near the *Fontana*, sitting in a little *trattoria*. He was dressed in check plus-fours with a green bush jacket and a cap with a peak. He was addressing a plate of spaghetti—and *do you know what?*"

"No. What?"

"There was a *Coca Cola* before him with a straw in it."

"Great heavens, Antrobus, you are jesting."

"My solemn oath, old man."

"It's the end."

"The very end. Poor Polk-Mowbray. I tried to cringe my way past him but he saw me and called out." Here Antrobus shuddered. "He said, quite distinctly, quite unequivocally, without a shadow of doubt—he said: '*Hiya!*' and made a sort of gesture in the air as of someone running his hand listlessly over the buttocks of a chorus girl. I won't imitate it in here, someone might see."

"I know the gesture you mean."

"Well," said Antrobus bitterly, "now you know the worst. I suppose it's a symptom of the age really." As we sauntered out of his club, acknowledging the porter's greeting with a nod, he put on his soft black hat and put his umbrella into the crook of his arm. His face had taken on its graven image look—"a repository of the nation's darkest secrets". We walked in silence for a while until we reached my bus stop. Then he said: "Poor Polk-Mowbray. In Coca Cola veritas what?"

"Indeed," I said. There could not be a better epitaph.

3

Frying the Flag

"Of course, if there had been any justice in the world," said Antrobus, depressing his cheeks grimly. "If we ourselves had shown any degree of responsibility, the two old ladies would have been minced, would have been incinerated. Their ashes would have been trampled into some Serbian field or scattered in the sea off some Dalmatian island, like Drool or Snot. Or they would have been sold into slavery to the Bogomils. Or just simply crept up on from behind and murdered at their typewriters. I used to dream about it, old man."

"Instead of which they got a gong each."

"Yes. Polk-Mowbray put them up for an M.B.E. He had a perverted sense of humour. It's the only explanation."

"And yet time softens so many things. I confess I look back on the old *Central Balkan Herald* with something like nostalgia."

"Good heavens," said Antrobus, and blew out his cheeks. We were enjoying a stirrup-cup at his club before

28

taking a turn in the park. Our conversation, turning as it always did upon our common experiences abroad in the Foreign Service, had led us with a sort of ghastly inevitability to the sisters Grope; Bessie and Enid Grope, joint editor-proprietors of the *Central Balkan Herald* (circulation 500). They had spent all their lives in Serbia, for their father had once been Embassy chaplain and on retirement had elected to settle in the dusty Serbian plains. Where, however, they had inherited the old flat-bed press and the stock of battered Victorian faces, I cannot tell, but the fact remains that they had produced between them an extraordinary daily newspaper which remains without parallel in my mind after a comparison with newspapers in more than a dozen countries—"THE BALKAN HERALD KEEPS THE BRITISH FLAG FRYING"—that was the headline that greeted me on the morning of my first appearance in the Press Department. It was typical.

The reason for a marked disposition towards misprints was not far to seek; the composition room, where the paper was hand-set daily, was staffed by half a dozen hirsute Serbian peasants with greasy elf-locks and hands like shovels. Bowed and drooling and uttering weird eldrich-cries from time to time they went up and down the type-boxes with the air of half-emancipated baboons hunting for fleas. The master printer was called Icic (pronounced Itchitch) and he sat forlornly in one corner living up to his name by scratching himself from time to time. Owing to such laborious methods of composition the editors were hardly ever able to call for extra proofs; even as it was the struggle to get the paper out on the streets was grandiose to watch. Some time in the early thirties it had come out a day late and that day had never been made up. With admirable single-mindedness the sisters decided, so as not to leave gaps in their files, to keep the date twenty-four hours behind reality until such times as, by a superhuman effort, they could produce two newspapers in one day and thus catch up.

Bessie and Enid Grope sat in the editorial room which was known as the "den". They were both tabby in colouring and wore rusty black. They sat facing one another pecking at two ancient typewriters which looked as if they had been obtained from the Science Museum of the Victoria and Albert.

. Bessie was News, Leaders, and Gossip; Enid was Features, Make-up and general Sub. Whenever they were at a loss for copy they would mercilessly pillage ancient copies of *Punch* or *Home Chat*. An occasional hole in the copy was filled with a ghoulish smudge—local block-making clearly indicated that somewhere a poker-work fanatic had gone quietly out of his mind. In this way the *Central Balkan Herald* was made up every morning and then delivered to the composition room where the chain-gang rapidly reduced it to gibberish. MINISTER FINED FOR KISSING IN PUBIC. WEDDING BULLS RING OUT FOR PRINCESS. QUEEN OF HOLLAND GIVES PANTY FOR EX-SERVICE MEN. MORE DOGS HAVE BABIES THIS SUMMER IN BELGRADE. BRITAINS NEW FLYING-GOAT.

In the thirties this did not matter so much but with the war and the growth of interest in propaganda both the Foreign Office and the British Council felt that an English newspaper was worth keeping alive in the Balkans if only to keep the flag flying. A modest subsidy and a free news service went a long way to help the sisters, though of course there was nothing to be done with the crew down in the composition room. "Mrs. Schwartkopf has cast off clothes of every description and invites

Vasiliu

inspection", "In a last desperate spurt the Cambridge crew, urged on by their pox, overtook Oxford".

Every morning I could hear the whistles and groans and sighs as each of the secretaries unfolded his copy and addressed himself to his morning torture. On the floor above, Polk-Mowbray kept drawing his breath sharply at every misprint like someone who has run a splinter into his finger. At this time the editorial staff was increased by the addition of Mr. Tope, an elderly catarrhal man who made up the news page, thus leaving Bessie free to follow her bent in paragraphs on gardening ("How to Plant Wild Bubs") and other extravagances. It was understood that at some time in the remotest past Mr. Tope had been in love with Bessie but he "had never Spoken"; perhaps he had fallen in love with both sisters simultaneously and had been unable to decide which to marry. At all events he sat in the "den" busy with the world news; every morning he called on me for advice. "We want the *Herald* to play its full part in the war effort," he never failed to assure me gravely. "We are all in this together." There was little I could do for him.

At times I could not help feeling that the *Herald* was more trouble than it was worth. References, for example, to "Hitler's nauseating inversion—the rocket-bomb" brought an immediate visit of protest from Herr Schpünk the German *chargé*, dictionary in hand, while the early stages of the war were greeted with BRITAIN DROPS BIGGEST EVER BOOB ON BERLIN. This caused mild speculation as to whom this personage might be. Attempts, moreover, to provide serious and authoritative articles for the *Herald* written by members of the Embassy shared the same fate. Spalding, the commercial attaché who was trying to negotiate on behalf of the British

Mining Industry, wrote a painstaking survey of the wood resources of Serbia which appeared under the startling banner BRITAIN TO BUY SERBIAN TIT-PROPS, while the the military attaché who was rash enough to contribute a short strategic survey of Suez found that the phrase "Canal Zone" was printed without a "C" throughout. There was nothing one could do. "One feels so desperately ashamed," said Polk-Mowbray, "with all the resources of culture and so on that we have—that a British newspaper abroad should put out such disgusting gibberish. After all, it's semi-official, the Council has subsidized it specially to spread the British Way of Life. . . . It's not good enough."

But there was nothing much we could do. The *Herald* lurched from one extravagance to the next. Finally in the columns of Theatre Gossip there occurred a series of what Antrobus called Utter Disasters. The reader may be left to imagine what the Serbian compositors would be capable of doing to a witty urbane and deeply considered review of the 100,000th performance of *Charley's Aunt*.

The *Herald* expired with the invasion of Yugoslavia and the sisters were evacuated to Egypt where they performed prodigies of valour in nursing refugees. With the return to Belgrade, however, they found a suspicious Communist régime in power which ignored all their requests for permission to refloat the *Herald*. They brought their sorrows to the Embassy, where Polk-Mowbray received them with a stagey but absent-minded sympathy. He agreed to plead with Tito, but of course he never did. "If they start that paper up again," he told his Chancery darkly, "I shall resign." "They'd make a laughing stork out of you, sir," said Spalding. (The pre-war mission had been returned almost unchanged.)

Mr. Tope also returned and to everyone's surprise had Spoken and had been accepted by Bessie; he was now comparatively affluent and was holding the post which in the old days used to be known as Neuter's Correspondent—aptly or not who can say?

"Well, I think the issue was very well compounded by getting the old girls an M.B.E. each for distinguished services to the British Way of Life. I'll never forget the investiture with Bessie and Enid in tears and Mr. Tope swallowing like a toad. And all the headlines Spalding wrote for some future issue of the *Herald*: 'Sister Roasted in Punk Champage after solemn investitute'."

"It's all very well to laugh," said Antrobus severely, "but a whole generation of Serbs have had their English gouged and mauled by the *Herald*. Believe me, old man, only yesterday I had a letter from young Babic, you remember him?"

"Of course."

"For him England is peppered with fantastic place-names which he can only have got from the *Herald*. He says he enjoyed visiting Henleg Regatta and Wetminster Abbey; furthermore, he was present at the drooping of the colour; he further adds that the noise of Big Bun striking filled him with emotion; and that he saw a film about Florence Nightingale called 'The Lade With the Lump'. No, no, old man, say what you will the *Herald* has much to answer for. It is due to sinister influences like the Gropes and Topes of this world that the British Council's struggle is such an uphill one. Care for another?"

34

Jots and Tittles

"In Diplomacy," said Antrobus, "quite small things can be One's Undoing; things which in themselves may be Purely Inadvertent. The Seasoned Diplomat keeps a sharp eye out for these moments of Doom and does what he can to avert them. Sometimes he succeeds, but sometimes he fails utterly—and then Irreparable Harm ensues.

"Foreigners are apt to be preternaturally touchy in small ways and I remember important negotiations being spoilt sometimes by a slip of the tongue or an imagined slight. I remember an Italian personage, for example (let us call him the Minister for Howls and Smells), who with the temerity of ignorance swarmed up the wrong side of the C.-in-C. Med.'s Flagship in Naples harbour with a bunch of violets and a bottle of Strega as a gift from the Civil Servants of Naples. He was not only ordered off in rather stringent fashion but passes were made at him with a brass-shod boathook. This indignity cost us dear and we practically had to resort to massage to set things right.

"Then there was the Finnish Ambassador's wife in Paris who slimmed so rigorously that her stomach took to rumbling quite audibly at receptions. I suppose she was hungry. But no sooner did she walk into a room with a buffet in it than her stomach set up growls of protest. She tried to pass it off by staring hard at other people but it didn't work. Of course, people not in the know simply thought that someone upstairs was moving furniture about. But at private dinner parties this characteristic was impossible to disguise; she would sit rumbling at her guests who in a frenzy of politeness tried to raise their voices above the noise. She soon lost ground in the Corps. Silences would fall at her parties—the one thing that Diplomats fear more than anything else. When silences begin to fall, broken only by the rumblings of a lady's entrails, it is The Beginning of the End.

"But quite the most illuminating example of this sort of thing occurred on the evening when Polk-Mowbray swallowed a moth. I don't think I ever told you about it before. It is the sort of thing one only talks about in the strictest confidence. It was at a dinner party given to the Communist People's Serbian Trade and Timber Guild sometime during Christmas week back in '49. Yugoslavia at that time had just broken with Stalin and was beginning to feel that the West was not entirely populated by 'capitalist hyenas' as the press said. They were still wildly suspicious of us, of course, and it was a very hot and embarrassed little group of peasants dressed in dark suits who accepted Polk-Mowbray's invitation to dinner at the Embassy. Most of them spoke only their mother tongue. Comrade Bobok, however, the leader of the delegation, spoke a gnarled embryonic English. He was a huge sweating Bosnian peasant with a bald head. His number two, Pepic, spoke the sort of French that one imagines is learned in mission houses in Polynesia. From a diplomatist's point of view they were Heavy Going.

"I shall say nothing about their messy food habits; Drage the butler kept circling the table and staring at them as if he had gone out of his senses. We were all pretty sweaty and constrained by the time the soup plates were removed. The conversation was early cave-man stuff consisting of growls and snarls and weird flourishes of knife and fork. Bobok and Pepic sat on Polk-Mowbray's right and left respectively; they were flanked by Spalding the Commercial Attaché and myself. We were absolutely determined to make the evening a success. De Mandeville for some curious reason best known to himself had decreed that we should eat turkey with mustard and follow it up with plum pudding. I suppose it was because it was Christmas week. Comrade Bobok fell foul of the mustard almost at once and only quenched himself by lengthy potations which, however, were all to the good as they put him into a good temper.

"The whole thing might have been carried off perfectly well had it not been for this blasted moth which had been circling the Georgian candlesticks since the start of the dinner-party and which now elected to get burnt and crawl on to Polk-Mowbray's side-plate to die. Polk-Mowbray himself was undergoing the fearful strain of decoding Comrade Bobok's weighty pleasantries which were full of corrupt groups and he let his attention wander for one fatal second.

"As he talked he absently groped in his side-plate for a piece of bread. He rolls bread balls incessantly at dinner, as you know. Spalding and I saw in a flash of horror something happen for which our long diplomatic training had not prepared us. Mind you, I saw a journalist eat a wine-glass once, and once in Prague I saw a Hindu diplomat's wife drain a glass of vodka under the impression that it was water. She let out a moan which still rings in my ears. But never in all my long service have I seen an Ambassador eat a moth—and this is precisely what Polk-Mowbray did. He has a large and serviceable mouth and into it Spalding and I saw the moth disappear. There was a breathless pause during which our poor Ambassador suddenly realized that something was wrong; his whole frame stiffened with a dreadful premonition. His large and expressive eye became round and glassy with horror.

"This incident unluckily coincided with two others; the first was that Drage walked on with a blazing pudding stuck with holly. Our guests were somewhat startled by this apparition, and Comrade Bobok, under the vague impression that the blazing pud must be ushering in a spell of diplomatic toasts, rose to his feet and cried loudly: 'To Comrade Tito and the Communist People's Serbian Trade and Timber Guild. *Jiveo!*' His fellow Serbs rose as one man and shouted: '*Jiveo!*'

"By this time, however, light had begun to dawn on Polk-Mowbray. He let out a hoarse jarring cry full of despair and charred moth, stood up, threw up his arms and groped his way to the carafe on the sideboard, shaken by a paroxysm of coughing. Spalding and I rocked, I am sorry to say, with hysterical giggles, followed him to pat him on the back. To the startled eyes of the Yugoslavs we must have presented the picture of three diplomats laughing ourselves to death and slapping each other on the back at the sideboard, and utterly ignoring the sacred toast. Worse still, before any of us could

turn and explain the situation Spalding's elbow connected with Drage's spinal cord. The butler missed his footing and scattered the pudding like an incendiary bomb all over the table and ourselves. The Yugoslav delegation sat there with little odd bits of pudding blazing in their laps or on their waistcoats, utterly incapable of constructive thought. Spalding, I am sorry to say, was racked with guffaws now which were infectious to a degree. De Mandeville who was holding the leg of the table and who had witnessed the tragedy also started to laugh in a shrill feminine register.

"I must say Polk-Mowbray rallied gamely. He took an enormous gulp of wine from the carafe and led us all back to table with apologies and excuses which sounded, I must say, pretty thin. What Communist could believe a capitalist hyena when he says that he has swallowed a moth? Drage was flashing about snuffing out pieces of pudding.

"We made some attempt to save the evening, but in vain. The awful thing was that whenever Spalding caught De Mandeville's eye they both subsided into helpless laughter. The Yugoslavs were in an Irremediable Huff and from then on they shut up like clams, and took their collective leave even before the coffee was served.

"It was quite clear that Spalding's Timber Pact was going to founder in mutual mistrust once more. The whole affair was summed up by the *Central Balkan Herald* in its inimitable style as follows: 'We gather that the British Embassy organized a special dinner at which the Niece de Resistance was Glum Pudding and a thoroughly British evening was enjoyed by all.' You couldn't say fairer than that, could you?"

5

For Immediate Release

"Most F.O. types", said Antrobus, "are rather apt to imagine that their own special department is more difficult to run than any other; but I must say that I have always handed the palm to you Information boys. It seems to me that Press work has a higher Horror Potential than any other sort."

He is right, of course. Antrobus is always right, and even though I am no longer a foreign service type I am proud to be awarded even this tardy recognition when all is said and done.

A press officer is like a man pegged out on an African ant-hill for the termites of the daily press to eat into at will. Nor are we ever decorated. You never read of a press officer getting the George Cross for rescuing a reporter who has fallen into his beer. Mostly we just sit around and look as if we were sickening for an O.B.E.

And what can compare with the task of making journalists feel that they are loved and wanted—without which they founder in the Oedipus Complex and start calling for a Parliamentary Commission to examine the Information Services? Say what you like, it's an unenviable job.

Most of the press officers I've known have gradually gone off their heads. I'm thinking of Davis who was found gibbering on the Nan Tal Pagoda in Bangkok. All he could say was: "For Immediate Release, absolutely immediate release." Then there was Perry who used to boil eggs over a spirit-lamp in the office. He ended by giving a press conference in his pyjamas.

But I think the nicest and perhaps the briefest press officer I have ever known was Edgar Albert Ponting. He was quite unique. One wonders how he was recruited into so select a cadre. He was sent to me as second secretary in Belgrade. I had been pressing for help for some time with a task quite beyond me. The press corps numbered some fifty souls—if journalists can be said to have souls. I could not make them all feel loved and wanted at once. Trieste with its ghastly possibilities of a shooting war loomed over us: propaganda alone, I was told, could keep the balance—could keep it a shouting war. I turned to the Foreign Office for help. Help came, with all the traditional speed and efficiency. After two months my eleventh telegram struck a sympathetic chord somewhere and I received the information that Edgar Albert was on the way. It was a great relief. Fraternization with the press corps had by this time raised my alcohol consumption to thirty *slivovitza* a day. People said they could see a pulse beating on the top of my head. My Ambassador had taken to looking at me in a queer speculative way, with his head on one side. It was touch and go. But it was splendid to know that help was at hand. It is only forty odd hours from London to Belgrade. Ponting would soon be at my elbow, mechanically raising and lowering his own with the old Fleet Street rhythm press officers learn so easily.

Mentally, I toasted Ponting in a glass of sparkling Alka Seltzer and called for the *Immediate* file. From Paris came the news that he had not been found on the train. After a wait of four days a signal came through saying that he had been found. He was at present in St. Anne's due for release later in the day when his journey would be resumed. I was rather uneasy as I remembered that St. Anne's was a mental hospital, but my fears subsided as I followed his route and saw him safely flagged into Switzerland and down into Italy. There was an ominous pause at Pisa which lasted ten days. Then came a signal from the Embassy in Rome saying that our vice-consul there had located him and put him on the train. This was followed by an odd sort of telegram from Ponting himself which said: *"Can't tell you what impression Leaning Tower made on me old man. On my way. Avanti. Ponty."*

At Venice there was another hold-up, but it was brief. Our vice-consul was away. It appeared that Ponting had borrowed 1,000 lire from the consulate gondolier and represented himself to the clerks in the consulate as a distressed British subject domiciled in Lisbon. All this was of course disquieting, but, as I say, one gets used to a highly developed sense of theatre in press officers. They live such drab lives. Once he was through Trieste and Zagreb, however, I began to breathe more freely, and make arrangements to meet him myself.

The Orient Express gets in at night. I had planned a quiet little dinner at the flat during which I would unburden myself to Ponting and brief him as to the difficulties which faced us. (A visit from the Foreign Minister impended: rumours of Russian troop movements were at meridian: trade negotiations with Britain were at a delicate phase: and so on and so forth.)

He was not at the station: my heart sank. But Babic, the Embassy chauffeur, interrogated the wagon-lit attendant, and we learned with relief that Ponting had indeed arrived. "He must have walked," said the attendant, "he had very little luggage besides the banjo. A little case like a lady's handbag."

We drove thoughtfully up the ill-paved streets of the capital and down Knez Mihailova to the only hotel set aside for foreign visitors (all the others had been turned into soup-kitchens and communal eating-houses). He was not at the hotel. I was standing at the desk, deep in thought, when the circular swing-doors of the hotel began to revolve, at first with slowness, then with an ever-increasing velocity which drew the eyes of the staff towards them. Somebody not too certain of his bearings was trying to get into the hotel. It seemed to me that he was rather over-playing his hand. By now the doors were going round so fast that one thought they would gradually zoom up through the ceiling, drawn by centrifugal force. Ponting was inside, trapped like a fly in amber. I caught sight of his pale self-deprecating face as he rotated grimly. It was set in an expression of forlorn desperation. How had this all come about? Could he have mistaken these massive mahogany doors for a bead curtain? Impossible to say. He was still holding his banjo to his bosom as he swept round and round. There was an impressive humming noise as of a nuclear reactor reacting, or of a giant top at full spin. Ponting looked dazed but determined, like a spinster trapped in a wind-tunnel. A small crowd of servants formed at a respectful distance to observe this phenomenon. Then without warning the second secretary was catapulted out of the swing-doors into our midst, like someone being fired out of a gun into a net. We recoiled with him, falling all over the staircase. For a brief moment his face expressed all the terror of a paralytic whose wheel chair has run away with him and is heading straight for the canal. Then he relaxed and allowed himself to be dusted down, gazing anxiously at his banjo all the time. "Thank God, Ponting, at last you're here," I said. I don't know why I should take the name of God in vain at a time like this; the words just slipped out.

He introduced himself in rather a mincing fashion. His eyes were certainly glassy. I put him down as a rather introverted type. I must say, however, that his opening remark "could not but" (as we say in despatches) fill me with misgiving. "This *slivovitza*," he said hoarsely, "it's a damn powerful thing. I'm practically clairvoyant, old man. You mustn't be shirty with old Ponting." He wagged a finger forlornly, helplessly. He looked as if he too needed to feel loved and wanted.

Physically he was on the small side, pigeon-chested and with longish arms which ended in fingers stained bright yellow with nicotine. He had the mournful innocent eyes of a mongrel. "Ponting," I said, "you'd better have a little rest before dinner." He did not protest, but leaning heavily against me in the lift he said under his breath, but with conviction: "If ever I get the Nobel Prize it won't be for nuclear physics." In my heart of hearts I could not help agreeing with him.

He laid himself out on his bed, kicked off his shoes, folded his arms behind his head, closed his eyes and said (in the veritable accents of Charlie McCarthy): "Quack. Quack. Quack. This is Ponting calling." Then in a different voice: "Did you say Ponting? Surely not Ponting."

Then reverting again to the dummy he so much resembled: "Yes Ponting. *The* Ponting, Ponting of Pontefract."

"Ponting," I said severely.

"Quack Quack," responded the dummy.

"Ponting, I'm going," I said.

He opened his eyes and stared wildly round him for a moment. "Is it true that the Ambassador lives on nightingale sandwiches?" he asked. There were tears in his eyes. "The *Daily Express* says so." I gave him a glance of cold dignity.

"I shall speak to you tomorrow," I said, "when you are sober." I meant it to sting.

By eleven o'clock next morning Ponting had not appeared and I sent the office car for him. He was looking vague and rather scared and had a large woollen muffler round his throat. His eyes looked as if they were on the point of dissolving, like coloured sweets. "Old man," he said hoarsely, "was there something you wanted?"

"I wanted to take you to H.E., but I can't take you looking like an old-clothes-man." He gazed down at himself in wonder. "What's wrong with me?" he said. "I bet you haven't got a shirt on under that scarf." I had already caught a glimpse of a pyjama jacket. "Well, anyway," said Ponting, "I can sign the book, can't I?"

I led him shambling through the Chancery to the Residence which I knew would be deserted at this hour. He made one or two hypnotist's passes at the Visitors' Book with streaming pen and finally delivered himself of a blob the size of a lemon. "It was the altitude," he explained. "My pen exploded in my pocket." I was busy mopping the ink with my handkerchief. "But you came by train," I said, with considerable exasperation, "not by air." Ponting nodded. "I mean the altitude of the Leaning Tower of Pisa," he said severely.

I led him back to the Chancery door. "Can I go back?" he asked humbly. "It takes a few days to acclimatize in a new post; H.E. won't be shirty with old Ponting, will he?"

"Go," I said, pointing a finger at the iron gates of the Embassy, "and don't come back until you are ready to do your job properly."

"Don't be shirty, old boy," he said reproachfully. "Ponting will see you through."

"Go," I said.

"In my last post," said Ponting in a brooding hollow sort of way, "they said I was afflicted with dumb insolence."

He traipsed down the drive to the waiting car, shaking his head sadly.

I was contorted with a hideous sense of desolation. What was to be done with a ventriloquist who played the banjo and spent half his time talking like a duck?

I went into the Chancery and took down the F.O. List to examine Ponting's background. His foreground had become only too apparent by now. He had had a number of posts, none of which he had held for more than a month or so; he had been moved round the world at breakneck speed, presumably leaving behind him in each town the indelible scars of a conduct which could only be excused by reference to the severest form of personality disorder. "Bitter fruit," I said to Potts the archivist. "Look at this character's record." He put on his spectacles and took the book from me. "Yes," he said. "In every post it would seem to be a case of retired hit-wicket. Poor Ponting!"

"Poor Ponting!" I said angrily. "Poor me!"

After that I did not see Ponting for several weeks. Once, late at night, my Head of Chancery surprised him in the lounge of his hotel doing a soft shoe routine and playing the banjo to a deeply attentive audience of partly sentient journalists. The heavy smell of plum brandy was in the air. In those days it cost about fourpence a glass. Ponting did a little song, a pitiful little spastic shuffle, and brought the performance to an end by pulling out his bow tie to the distance of a yard before letting it slap back on to his dicky. Antrobus, then first secretary, witnessed all this with speechless wonder. "By God," he said fervently, "never have I seen an Embassy let down like this. He popped his cheek at me in a dashed familiar fashion and said he had once acted in a pierrot troupe on Clacton pier. I couldn't bring him to his senses. He was . . ." words failed him. He reported the matter to H.E. who, from the armoury of his diplomatic experience, produced the word which had eluded Antrobus. "Bizarre," he said gravely. "I gather this fellow Ponting is a little bizarre."

"Yes, sir," I said.

"It's awfully peculiar," he said. "Your predecessor was an Oxford Grouper. He was bizarre too. At press conferences he would jump up and testify to the most awful sins. Finally the press protested." He paused. "If you don't mind my saying so," he said, "a large proportion of the Information Section in the F.O. seems a bit . . . well, bizarre." I could see that he was wondering rather anxiously what my particular form of mental trouble might be.

"I'm afraid Ponting will have to go."

"Well, if you say so. But as he's been civil enough to

sign the book I must give him a meal before he leaves."

"It would be unwise, sir."

"Nevertheless I will, poor fellow. You never know what he has on his mind."

"Very good, sir."

From then on Ponting became a sort of legendary figure. I tried to find him from time to time but he never seemed to be in. Once he phoned me to say that he was taking up a lot of contacts he had made and that I was not to worry about him. He had made a hit with the press, he added, everybody loved old Ponting and wanted him. I was so speechless with annoyance I forgot to tell him that telegrams suggesting his recall had already been sent to the Foreign Office. One day Antrobus came to my office; he appeared to be within an ace of having a severe internal haemorrhage. "This man Ponting", he exploded, "must be got out of the country. Britain's good name. . . ." He became absolutely incoherent.

"What's he done now?" I asked. Antrobus for once was not very articulate. He had met Ponting, dressed as a Roman centurion, walking down the main street of the town at twelve noon that morning. He had been, it seemed, to a fancy dress ball given by the Yugoslav ballet and was on his way back to his hotel. "He was reeling," said Antrobus, "absolutely reeling and speechless. Rubber lips, you know. Couldn't articulate. And the bastard popped his cheek at me again. And gave me a wink. Such a wink." He shuddered at the memory. "And that's not all," said Antrobus, his voice becoming shriller. "That's by no means all. He rang Eliot at three o'clock in the morning and said that H.E. didn't understand the Trieste problem and that he, Ponting, was going to open unilateral negotiations with Tito in his own name. I gather he was prevented by the tommy gunners on Tito's front door from actually carrying out his threat. Mark me, we shall hear more of this." Ponting's future never looked darker. That afternoon we got a call from the Ministry of Foreign Affairs. They wished to deliver an *aide mémoire* to the Embassy. Montacute went. He was the new Counsellor. He came back an hour later mopping his brow. "They say Ponting is a Secret Service agent. Unless we withdraw him he'll be declared *persona non grata*." I gave a sigh of relief. "Good. This will force the F.O.'s hand. I'll get off an Immediate." I did. The answer came back loud and clear that evening: "*Edgar Albert Ponting posted to Helsinki to leave by earliest available means.*"

Armed with this telegram I set out to find him. He was not at the hotel, nor at the only two restaurants available for foreigners. He was not at the Press Club though Garrick of the *Mirror*, who was expiating his sense of frustration in triple *slivovitzas*, told me he'd seen him. "He was trapped in the lift some hours ago. Dunno where he went afterwards." I finally ran him to earth in a Balkan *bistro* with an unpronounceable name. He was sitting at the bar with a girl on each side. His face was lifted to the ceiling and he was singing in a small bronchial voice:

> *I'm the last one left on the corner,*
> *There wasn't a girl for me,*
> *The one I loved married anovver,*
> *Yes anovver, yes anovver,*
> *Oo took 'er far over the sea.*

He was so moved by his own performance that he began to cry now, huge round almost solid tears which rained down and marked the dusty bar. This sort of behaviour is fairly normal among Serbs whenever they are drunk and the tragedy of The Great Panslav idea comes to mind. The girls patted him sympathetically on the back. "Poor old Ponty," said Ponting in hollow self-commiserating tones. "Nobody understands Ponty. Never felt loved and wanted." He blew his nose insanely in a dirty handkerchief and drained his glass. This cheered him. He said in a good strong cockney voice:

> *Come fill me with the old familiar jewce*
> *Mefinks I shall feel better bye and bye . . .*

"Ponting," I said. "There's some news for you."

He took the telegram in shaking fingers and read it out slowly like a peasant reading the Creed. "What's it mean?" he said.

"You're off tomorrow. There's a crisis in Helsinki which brooks of no delay. Ponting, the F.O. have chosen *you*. Your country is calling."

"Ta ra ra ra," he said irreverently and stood to the salute. We were all irresistibly impelled to do the same, the Serbian girls, the bartender and myself. It was the last memory I was to carry away of Ponting. I have often thought of him, and always with affection and respect. Some years ago I saw that he had transferred to the Colonial Office, and from that day forward, believe it or not, you could hardly open a newspaper without reading about a crisis in the colony where Ponting happened to be posted. Maybe it's only the sheer momentum of Ponting's influence which is pushing the Empire downhill at such a speed. I shouldn't be at all surprised.

White Man's Milk

"The Grape," said Antrobus with a magisterial air as he stared into the yellow heart of his Tio Pepe, "the Grape is a Rum Thing. I should say it was the Diplomat's Cross —just as I should say that in diplomacy a steady hand is an indispensable prerequisite to doing a job well. . . . Eh? The tragedies I've seen, old boy; you'd never credit them."

"Ponting?"

"Well, yes—but I wasn't even thinking of the element of Human Weakness. But just think of the varieties of alcoholic experience which are presented to one in the Foreign Service. To take one single example—National Days."

"My God, yes."

"To drink vodka with Russians, champagne with the French, *slivovitz* with Serba, *saki* with Japs, whisky and Coca Cola with the Yanks . . . the list seems endless. I've seen many an Iron Constitution founder under the strain. Some get pooped by one drink more than another. There was a Vice-Consul called Pelmet in Riga. . . ."

"Horace Pelmet?"

"Yes."

"But he didn't drink much, did he?"

"No. But there was one drink which he couldn't take at all. Schnapps. Unluckily he was posted to Riga and then Oslo. At first he was all right. He used to get slightly dappled, that was all. Then he started to get progressively pooped. Finally he became downright marinated. Always crashing his car or trying to climb the sentries outside the Embassy. We managed to hush things up as best we could and he might have held out until he got a transfer to a wine-growing post. But what finished him was a ghastly habit of ending every sentence with a shout whenever he was three or four schnapps down wind. You'd be at a perfectly serious reception exchanging Views with Colleagues when all of a sudden he'd start. You'd hear him say—he started quite low in the scale—"As far as I, Pelmet, am concerned"—and then suddenly ending in a bellow: "British policy IS A BLOODY CONUNDRUM." I heard him do this fourteen times in one evening. The German Minister protested. Of course, poor Pelmet had to go. They held him *en disponsibilité* for a year or so but no Chief of Mission would touch him. He died of a broken heart I believe. Took to wood-alcohol on a big scale. Poor fellow! Poor fellow!"

He sighed, drained his glass and raised a long finger in the direction of the bar for reinforcements. Merlin the steward replenished the glasses silently and withdrew.

"But the unluckiest chap of all", continued Antrobus after a short pause, "was undoubtedly Kawaguchi, the Jap Minister in Prague. His downfall was Quite Unforeseen. Poor chap."

"Tell me about him."

"His was a mission of some delicacy. He started off frightfully well. Indeed, they were an enchanting couple, the Kawaguchis. They spoke nothing but Jap, of course, which sounds like someone sand-papering a cheese-wire. With the rest of the Corps they were silent. Both were tiny and pretty as squirrels. Their features looked as if they had been painted on to papier mâché with a fine brush. At functions they sat together, side by side, holding on to their own wrists and saying nothing. But they were full of the small conventional diplomatic politeness —always sending round presents of sweets or paper fans with 'Made in Hong Kong' printed on them. Once I saw her laugh—she made a funny clicking sound. As for him, I don't honestly know how he conducted his business with the Czechs. There was some sort of trade pact being discussed at the time. Perhaps he used telepathy. Or perhaps he'd discovered some sort of Central European tic-tac. His whole mission consisted of two typist-clerks and a butler, none of whom spoke Czech. Anyway the important thing is this: the Kawaguchis never drank anything but *saki* which they imported in little white stone bottles. As you know it's a sort of brew from millet or something. . . ."

"Salty and mildly emetic."

"Yes: well, when they had to go out to a banquet or rout he always sent his butler over in the afternoon with a few small bottles of the stuff which were always placed before him at table. It was a familiar sight to see the two of them sitting there with their *saki* bottles before them. And so it was on this fatal evening which I am about to describe to you. It was New Year's Eve, I think: yes, and the French had elected to give a party. They always did things better than anyone else. The Kawaguchis were

WHITE MAN'S MILK

there, sitting in a corner, looking about them with their usual air of dazed benevolence. It was late and the party was in full swing. The usual petty scandals had enjoyed their usual public manifestation—the wife of the Finnish Consul had gone home in a huff because her husband had disappeared into the garden with the wife of the French First Secretary. A Russian diplomat was being sick in the Gentlemen's cloakroom. A nameless military attaché was behaving foully . . . we won't go into that. The general nostalgia had afflicted the band and a whole set of Old Viennese Waltzes was being played non-stop. As you know, it is a jolly difficult dance and can verge on the lethal. I always take cover when I hear 'The Blue Danube' coming up, old man."

"So do I."

"Well, imagine my astonishment when I saw the Kawaguchis rise from their chairs. They had never been known to dance, and at first I thought they were leaving. But something curious in their attitude drew my attention. They were gazing at the dancers like leopards. They both looked dazed and concentrated—as if they had been attending an ether party. Then he suddenly seized her round the waist and they began to dance, to the astonishment and delight of everyone. And they danced perfectly—a real Viennese waltz, old man, impeccable. I felt like cheering.

"They went round the floor once and then twice: everything under control. Then, old man, a ghastly premonition of the worst came over me, I can't tell why. Was it an optical illusion or were they dancing a bar or two faster than the music? I waited in an agony of impatience for them to come round again. It was only too true. They were one bar, two bars out of time. But their spin was absolute perfection still. By now, of course, the

56

Vasiliu

band began to feel the squeeze and increased the time. Indeed, the whole thing speeded up. But as fast as they overtook the Kawaguchis the faster did the two little Japs revolve. Perhaps in some weird Outer Mongolian way they thought it was all a race. I don't know. But I, who know the dangers and pitfalls of the Old Viennese Waltz, felt my throat contract with sympathy for them. There was no way one could help. A terrible blackness of soul came over me—for all his Czech colleagues were there on the floor dancing with their wives. It could only be a matter of time now. . . . The speed had increased to something like the Farnborough Air Show. Lots of people had dropped out but the floor was still quite full. The Kawaguchis were still travelling a dozen light-years ahead of the band, and the band with popping eyes was pumping and throbbing at its instruments in an attempt to catch them up. But by now they were no longer a dancing couple. They were a Lethal Weapon."

Antrobus paused and lit a cigarette with a shaking hand. Then he went on sadly. "The first to go was the Czech Minister of Finance, with whom Kawaguchi had been doing so frightfully well in negotiation. There was a sudden sharp crack and the next moment he was sitting on a violinist's knee holding his ankle while his wife stood ineffectually beating the air for a moment before subsiding on top of him. The Kawaguchis noticed nothing. They were in a trance. On they went. A series of collisions, trifling in themselves, now began to take place. The Chief Economic Adviser to the Treasury, Comrade Cicic, was dancing with a wife whose massive proportions and enormous buffer constituted a dance floor hazard at the best of times. In a waltz it was hair-raising to image what might happen.

"I calculated that if the Kawaguchis struck her they would certainly be halted dead. Not a bit of it. This frail little couple had achieved such a terrific momentum that when they struck Mrs. Cicic there was a dull crash only: a powder-compact in her evening bag exploded causing a cloud of apparent smoke to rise. When it cleared Mrs. and Mr. Cicic were reeling into the corner while the Kawaguchis were speeding triumphantly on their way. They had entered into the spirit of the waltz so deeply now that they were dancing with their eyes closed. There was something Inscrutably Oriental about the whole thing. I don't remember ever being so excited in my life. I began to tick off the casualties on my fingers. By now there were quite a number of walking-wounded and one or two near-stretcher cases; everywhere one could hear the astonished whispers of the Corps: 'C'est Kawaguchi qui l'a fait. . . .' 'Das ist Kawaguchi. . . .' But on they went, scattering destruction, and perhaps they would be going on still had not someone deflected them.

"I still don't quite remember how. All I remember is that all of a sudden they were off the floor and moving through the tables and chairs with the remorselessness of a snow-plough. At the end of the ballroom there were some tall french windows which were open. They opened on to a long terrace at the end of which there was an ornamental lake in the most tasteless post-Versailles tradition. Nevertheless. The Kawaguchis vanished through the french windows like a meteor, and such was the dramatic effect they had created that everyone rushed out after them just to see what would happen, including the band which was somehow still playing. It was just as if someone at a children's party had shouted: 'Come and look at the fireworks.' We all poured out on the terrace shouting and gesticulating. The Spanish Ambassador was shouting: 'For God's sake stop them. STOP THEM. Dio Mio!' But there wasn't any stopping them.

"The tragic but unbelievably beautiful momentum of their waltz had carried them into the shallow lake. Normally it would be snowbound but Prague had had a thaw this year. They sat, utterly exhausted but somehow triumphant in a foot of water and stench, smiling up at their colleagues of the Corps. The cold night air and the water which enveloped them seemed to be having a calming effect, but they made no effort to get out of the pond. They just stared and smiled quaintly. It was only then that I realized they were both drunk, old man. Absolutely pooped. People had come with lights now, and Czech doctors and alienists had appeared from everywhere. There were even some members of the Czech Red Cross with blankets and stretchers.

"We waded into the swamp to recover our colleague and his wife and after a bit of argument emptied them both into stretchers. I shall never forget her smile of sheer beatitude. Kawaguchi's face expressed only a Great Peace. As they bore him off I heard him say, more to himself than anyone: 'Oriental man different from White Man.' I have always remembered and treasured that remark, old boy. Something like the same thing was said by the French chargé's wife: 'How your Keepling say: "Ist is Ist and Vest is Vest"?' But I was sorry for the Kawaguchis. Magnificent as the whole thing was, here we were, with three minutes to go before midnight, simply covered in mud and confusion. Some of the women had tried to draw attention to themselves by rushing into the swamp after them. The Italian Ambassador had a sort of Plimsoll line in the middle of his dress trousers. The ballroom looked like an advance dressing-station on the Somme. It is impossible to pretend that the evening wasn't ruined. And above all, the dreadful smell. Apparently all the drains flowed into this romantic little lake. It was all very well so long as it wasn't disturbed. The French were definitely confused, and I for one was sorry for them. No Mission could carry off a thing like this lightly."

Antrobus blew out his cheeks and lay back in his armchair, keeping a watchful eye on me to see that I had fully appreciated all the points in the drama. Then he went on in his usual churchwarden's style: "The Kawaguchis left for Tokyo by air the next afternoon. His mission was a failure and he knew it. I must say that there were only two Colleagues at the airport to see him off—myself and the perfectly foul military attaché about whom I will never be persuaded to speak. He was deeply moved that we had troubled to find out the time of his departure from the Protocol. I wrung his hand. I knew he wasn't to blame for the whole thing. I knew it was purely Inadvertent."

"How do you mean?"

"The butler gave the whole thing away some weeks later. Apparently the normal case of *saki* had not come in that month. They were out of drink. There was nothing a responsible butler of any nationality could do. He took some of the *saki* bottles and filled them with . . . guess what?"

"Bad Scotch whisky."

"Dead right! 'White Man's Milk' he called it."

"Awfully bad luck."

"Of course. But we face these hazards in the Foreign Service, don't we?"

"Of course we do."

WHITE MAN'S MILK

"And we outlive them. Kawaguchi is in Washington."

"Bravo! I'm so glad."

"Care for another whiff of Grape-Shot before we lunch?"

7

Drage's Divine Discontent

"Did I ever tell you about the time when Drage, the Embassy butler, began to suffer from visions? No? Well, it was dashed awkward for all concerned and Polk-Mowbray was almost forced to Take Steps at the end.

"You probably remember Drage quite well: a strange, craggy Welsh Baptist with long curving arms as hairy as a Black Widow. A moody sort of chap. He had a strange way of gnashing his dentures when he spoke on religious matters until flecks of foam appeared at the corners of his mouth. For many years he had been a fairly devout fellow and always took a prominent part in things like servants' prayers. He also played the harmonium by ear at the English church—a performance to be carefully avoided on Sundays. For the rest one always found him hunched over a penny Bible in the buttery when he should have been cleaning the M. of W. silver. His lips moved and he made a deep purring sound in his throat as he read. We were all, frankly, rather scared of Drage.

"The awful thing about him was that he wore a wig

so obvious that he gave one the impression of having just stepped off the stage after a successful performance as Caliban. It was an indeterminate badger-grey affair which left a startling pink line across his forehead. The gum-like colour of the integument simply didn't match the rocky blueish skin of his face. Everyone knew it was a wig. Nobody ever dared to say so or allude to it.

"As for the visions, he confessed later that they had been gaining on him for some considerable time, and if he never mentioned them before it was because he felt that once we all recognized him as the Lord's Anointed we might give him the sack, or at least ask him to step down in favour of Bertram the footman. As you see, there were flashes of reason in the man. But all this intense Bible-squeezing could not help but have an effect on him, and one night at a party given for the Dutch Ambassador he dropped his tray and pointed with shaking finger at the wall behind Polk-Mowbray's head, crying in the parched voice of an early desert father: 'Here they come, sor, in all their glory! Just behind you, sor, Elijah up, as sure as I'm standing here!' He then covered his eyes as if blinded by the vision and fell mumbling to his knees.

"While in one sense one felt privileged to be present at Drage's Ascension into Heaven by fiery chariot, nevertheless his timing seemed inconsiderate. First of all poor Polk-Mowbray sprang to his feet and overturned his chair. Our guests were startled. Then to make things worse the Naval Attaché who dabbled in the occult and who hated to be left out of anything pretended to share Drage's vision. I think he had been drinking pink gins. He pointed his finger and echoed the butler. 'There they go!' he said in cavernous tones. 'Behind you!'

Vasiliu

" 'What the deuce is it?' said Polk-Mowbray nervously, seating himself once more, but gingerly.

"Benbow slowly moved his pointing finger as he traced the course of the Heavenly Host round the dining-room table. 'So clear I can actually touch them,' he said. He was now pointing at De Mandeville who had changed colour. He leaned forward and touched the Third Secretary's ear-lobe. De Mandeville gave a squeak.

"As you can imagine the whole atmosphere of our dinner party was subtly strained after this. Bertram led Drage off into the wings in a rather jumbled state and bathed his brow from a champagne bucket. Benbow was sent to Coventry by common consent. Nevertheless, he spent the rest of the evening in high good humour, occasionally pointing his finger and saying indistinctly: 'Here they come again.' He kept the Dutch looking over their shoulders.

"Naturally, one could not tolerate visions during meals and when Drage recovered Polk-Mowbray told him to cut it out or leave. The poor butler was deeply troubled. Apparently he had discovered that he had never been baptized and this was preying on his mind. 'Well,' said Polk-Mowbray, 'if you think baptism will cure you of visions I can easily arrange with Bishop Toft to give you a sprinkle. He arrives next week.'

"Twice a year the Bishop of Malta came in for a couple of days to marry, baptize or excommunicate the members of the Embassy living in exile amidst the pagan Yugoslavs. He was, as you remember, a genial and worldly bishop, but hopelessly absent-minded. He brought in with him a sort of acolyte called Wagstaffe who was spotty and adenoidal and did the washing-up of thuribles or whatever acolytes have to do. He was simply Not There as far as the Things Of This World are concerned. He was a Harrovian. It stuck out a mile. Well, this year the bishop's visit coincided with that of Brigadier Dilke-Parrot. In fact they came in the same car and stood being noisily genial in the hall as their bags were unstrapped. The brigadier, who was large and red and had moustaches like antlers, also came every year on some mysterious mission which enabled him to have two days' shooting on the snipe-marshes outside the town. He always brought what he was pleased to call his '*Bundook*' with him—a twelve-bore by Purdy. This year there appeared to be two gun-cases—pay attention to this—and the second one belonged to the bishop. It contained a magnificent episcopal crook, taller when all the bits were screwed together than the bishop himself. These two very similar cases lay side by side in the hall. Thereby hangs my tale.

"Drage greeted Bishop Toft with loud cries of delight and weird moppings and mowings and tugs at his forelock. He explained his case and the bishop rather thoughtfully agreed to baptize him. But here there was an unexpected hitch: Drage refused to be baptized in his wig; he wanted to feel the Jordan actually flowing on his cranium, so it was agreed that the baptism should take place in the privacy of the buttery where the butler could reveal all. A drill was worked out. After the ceremony Drage would replace his foliage and the bishop would then walk ahead of him, holding his crook, to the ballroom where the rest of the Embassy staff would be waiting to receive his ministrations. There were half a dozen babies to baptize that year.

"Well, Drage knelt down, and there was a tearing noise like old canvas. A large polished expanse of dome was presented to the bishop. He said afterwards that he blenched rather because Drage looked so extraordinary. Bits of dry glue were sticking to his scalp here and there. Well, the Bishop of Malta was just about to read the good news and anoint the butler when Wagstaffe opened the leather case and found that it contained the brigadier's '*bundook*'. It was imperative to acquaint the bishop with this mishap as he could hardly walk into the crowded Embassy ballroom holding a shotgun like a hillbilly. But how to interrupt Toft who by now was in mid-per-oration? Wagstaffe had always been an irresolute person. He could hardly call out: 'Hey, look at this for an epis-copal crook.' He fitted the barrel and stock together with the vague idea of holding it up for the bishop to see. He did not look to see if it was loaded. He started working his way stealthily round the kneeling Drage to where he might catch the bishop's eye.

"But it was the eye of the butler which first lighted on the weapon. He had always been a suspicious person and now it seemed as clear as daylight that while the bishop was holding him in thrall Wagstaffe had orders to stalk him from behind and murder him. Perhaps the shot would be a signal for the massacre of Baptists everywhere. Drage's Welsh heritage came to the surface multiplying his suspicions. And to think that this silver-haired old cleric went about getting Baptists murdered. . . . A hoarse cry escaped his lips.

"The irresolute acolyte started guiltily, and as Drage scrambled to his feet, he dropped the gun on to the carpet where it went off. The brigadier had always boasted of its hair-trigger action.

"The dull boom in the buttery sounded frightfully loud to the rest of us in the ballroom across the corridor.

It was followed by a spell of inarticulate shouting and then all of a sudden Drage appeared, running backwards fairly fast, pursued by the bishop with his sprinkler, making vaguely reassuring gestures and noises. Wagstaffe staggered to the door deathly pale and fainted across the two front rows of as yet unbaptized babes. They set up a dreadful concert of frightened screams.

"It was a dreadful scene as you can imagine. Drage disappeared into the garden and was only persuaded to come back and finish his baptism by the united efforts of Benbow, De Mandeville and myself. Moreover, he felt humiliated to be seen wigless by the whole Embassy. It took some time to straighten things out, specially as the mud-stained brigadier had by now arrived in a fearful temper, holding the episcopal crook between finger and thumb with an expression of the deepest distaste on his face.

"But as it happens things turned out very well. A pair of bright brown eyes had observed the downfall of Drage. To Smilija, the second housemaid, Drage's baldness seemed a wonderful thing. She had never realized how beautiful he could be until she saw his cranium taking the sunlight. It was a revelation and love now entered where formerly indifference only was. . . . They are married now; the visions have stopped; his wig has been sold as a prop to the Opera Company. You occasionally see it in the chorus of *Parsifal*. Which illustrates another little contention of mine: namely that Everybody Is Somebody's Cup Of Tea. Another one before we dine?"

8

"Noblesse Oblige"

"The case of Aubrey de Mandeville is rather an odd one.
I often wonder what the poor fellow is doing now. He
wasn't cut out for Diplomacy—indeed it puzzles me to
think how Personnel Branch could have considered him
in any way the answer to a maiden's prayer at all. It was
all due to Polk-Mowbray's folly, really."

"I don't remember him."

"It was the year before you came."

"Polk-Mowbray was Ambassador?"

"Yes. He'd just got his K.C.M.G. and was feeling
extremely pleased about it. He'd invited his niece Angela
to spend the summer at the Embassy and it was I think
this factor which preyed on his mind. This Angela was
rather a wild young creature—and as you know there was
not much to do in Communist Yugoslavia in those days.
I think he rather feared that she would fall in with a hard-
drinking Serbian set and set the Danube on fire. His
dearest wish was that she should marry into the Diplomatic, so he hit upon a brilliant scheme. He would order

70

someone suitable through Personnel and do a bit of match-making. Scott-Peverel the Third Secretary was married. He would have him replaced by Angela's hypothetical Intended. A dangerous game, what? I warned him when I saw the letter. He wanted, he said, a Third Secretary, Eton and Caius, aged 25 (approx.), of breeding and some personal fortune, who could play the flute. (At this time he was mad about an Embassy Quartet which met every week to fiddle and scrape in the Residence.) He must have known that you can't always depend on Personnel. However, despite my admonitions he sent the letter off and put the wheels in motion for Bunty Scott-Peverel's transfer to Tokyo. That was how we got De Mandeville. On paper he seemed to fill the bill adequately, and when his Curriculum Vitae came Polk-Mowbray was rather disposed to crow over me. But I kept my own counsel. I had Doubts, old boy, Grave Doubts.

"They were unshaken even by his personal appearance ten days later, sitting bolt upright in the back of a Phantom Rolls with the De Mandeville arms stencilled on the doors. He was smoking a cheroot and reading the Racing Calendar with close attention. His chauffeur was unloosing a cataract of white pig-skin suitcases, each with a gold monogram on it. It was quite clear that he was a *parvenu*, old boy. Moreover the two contending odours he gave off were ill-matched—namely gin-fumes and violet-scented hair lotion of obviously Italian origin. He condescendingly waved a ringed hand at me as I introduced myself. It had been, he said, a nerve-racking journey. The Yugoslavs had been so rude at the border that poor Dennis had cried and stamped his foot. Dennis was the chauffeur. 'Come over, darling, and be introduced to the Man,' he cried. The chauffeur was called Dennis Purfitt-

71

Purfitt. You can imagine my feelings, old man. I felt a pang for poor Polk-Mowbray and not less for Angela who was lying upstairs in the Blue Bedroom sleeping off a hangover. 'Dennis is my pianist as well as my chauffeur,' said De Mandeville as he dismounted holding what looked like a case of duelling pistols but which later turned out to be his gold-chased flute.

"I must confess that I was a bit gravelled for conversational matter with De Mandeville. 'I'll take you to meet H.E. at eleven,' I said huskily, 'if you would like time for a rest and a wash. You will be staying a night or two in the Residence until your flat is ready.'

" 'Anything you say, darling boy,' he responded, obviously determined to be as agreeable as he knew how. In my mind's eye I could see Angela weeping hot salt tears into her pillow after her first meeting with De Mandeville. It was just another of Personnel's stately little miscalculations. However, I held my peace and duly presented him all round. His interview with Polk-Mowbray lasted about fifteen seconds. Then my telephone rang: Polk-Mowbray sounded incoherent. It is clear that he had received a Mortal Blow. 'This ghastly fellow,' he spluttered. I tried to soothe him. 'And above all,' said Polk-Mowbray, 'impress on him that no Ambassador can tolerate being addressed as "darling boy" by his Third Secretary.' I told De Mandeville this with a good deal of force. He curled his lip sadly and picked his nose. 'Now you've hurt little Aubrey,' he said reproachfully. 'However,' and he drew himself together adding: 'Little Aubrey mustn't pout.' You can imagine, old boy, how I felt.

"De Mandeville's job as Third Secretary was largely social, looking after appointments and visitors and arranging *placements*. I could not help trembling for Polk-Mowbray. The new Third Secretary would sit there at his desk taking snuff out of a gold-chased snuff-box and reading despatches through a huge magnifying glass. He was a *numéro* all right.

"His first act was to paint his flat peacock blue and light it with Chinese lanterns. He and the chauffeur used to sit about in Russian shirts under a sun-lamp playing nap or manicuring their nails. Angela went steadily into a decline. Once when he was an hour late for dinner at the Embassy he excused himself by saying that he had gone upstairs to change his rings and had been simply unable to decide which to wear. He used to have his hair waved and set every month, and made the mistake of going to a Serbian hairdresser to have it done. You know how game the Serbs are, old man? Terribly willing. Will always do their best. They waved De Mandeville's hair into the crispest bunch of curls you are ever likely to see outside Cruft's. It was ghastly. Polk-Mowbray was almost beside himself. He wrote a long offensive letter to Personnel accusing them of sending out a steady stream of female impersonators to foreign posts and smirching the British name, etc.

"De Mandeville himself seemed impervious to criticism. He just pouted. So long as he confined his social activities to his own sphere he was not dangerous. But as time went on he found the diplomatic round rather boring and decided to take the Embassy in hand. His *placements* became more vivid. He also began a series of ill-judged experiments with the Residency Menus. Some of the more nauseating local edibles found their way on to the Embassy sideboards under stupefying French names. I remember a dinner at which those disgusting Dalmatian sea slugs were served, labelled '*Slugs Japonaises au Gratin*'. The naval attaché went down after this meal with a prolonged nervous gastritis. A Stop Had To Be Put to De Mandeville; of course by now Polk-Mowbray was working night and day to have him replaced—but these things take time.

"Meanwhile the Third Secretary swam in the diplomatic pool in a hair net, took a couple of Siamese kittens for walks with him on a lead, and smoked cigarettes in a holder so long that it was always catching in things.

"His final feat of *placement*—he was dealing with central European Politburo members of equal rank—was to have the Embassy dining-table cut in half and a half-moon scooped out of each end. When it was fitted together again there was a hole in the middle for H.E. to sit in while his guests sat round the outer circle. Polk-Mowbray was furious. He suffers terribly from claustrophobia and to be hemmed in by this unbroken circle of ape-like faces was almost more than flesh and blood could stand.

"On another occasion De Mandeville dressed all the waiters in Roman togas with laurel wreaths: this was to honour the twenty-first birthday of the Italian Ambassador's daughter. On the stroke of midnight he arranged for a flock of white doves to be released—he had hidden them behind screens. Well, this would have been all right except for one Unforeseen Contingency. The doves flew up as arranged and we were all admiration at the spectacle. But the poor creatures took fright at the lights and the clapping and their stomachs went out of order. They flew dispiritedly round and round the room involuntarily bestowing the Order of the Drain Second Class on us all. You can imagine the scene. It took ages to shoo them through the french windows into the garden. The Roman

waiters had to come on with bowls and sponges and remove the rather unorthodox decorations we all appeared
to be wearing.

"But the absolute *comble* was when, without warning
anyone, he announced that there would be a short
cabaret to amuse the Corps at a reception in honour of
Sir Claud Huft, the then Minister of State. The cabaret
consisted of De Mandeville and his chauffeur dressed as
Snow Maidens. They performed a curious and in some
ways rather spirited dance ending in an abandoned *can-
can*. It was met with wild applause: but not from Polk-
Mowbray as you can imagine. He found the whole
episode Distasteful and Unacceptable. De Mandeville
left us complete with pigskin suitcases, flute-case, and
chauffeur in the Great Rolls. We were all quite dry-eyed
at the leave-taking. But it seemed to me then that there
was a Moral to be drawn from it all. Never trust Personnel Branch, old man.

"As for poor Angela she was in sad case. Polk-
Mowbray sent her to Rome for the Horse Show and—
guess what? She up and married a groom. It was a sort
of involuntary rebound in a way. Everyone was spell-
bound with shame. But she had the good sense to go off
to Australia with him, where I gather that one needs little
Protective Colouring, and there they are to this day. The
whole thing, old man, only goes to show that You Can't
Be Too Careful."

9

Call of the Sea

"I have never really respected Service Attachés," said Antrobus. "Some I have known have bordered on the Unspeakable—like that ghastly Trevor Pope-Pope. I don't know how he got into the Blues, nor why he was ever posted to us. He used to lock himself into the cipher-room and play roulette all day with the clerks. Skinned them all, right and left. He had no mercy on anyone. He also used to sell bonded champagne by the case to dis-agreeable Latin-American Colleagues for pesos. And to cap it all the fellow wore embroidered bedsocks.

"But as for 'Butch' Benbow, he was one of the least objectionable service postings. He was naval attaché, you remember."

"Yes."

"The fact that he was so decent makes the whole epi-sode inexplicable. I really cannot decide in my own mind whether he did sever that tow-rope or not. And yet I saw him with my own eyes. So did Spalding. Yet the whole thing seems out of keeping with Benbow. But who knows what obscure promptings may stir the heart of a naval attaché condemned to isolation in Belgrade, hundreds of dusty miles from the sound of the sea? And then, imagine being designated to a country with almost no recognizable fleet. There was nothing for him to do once he had counted the two ex-Japanese condemned destroyers and the three tugs which made up Yugoslavia's quota of naval strength. Nor can the horse-drawn barges on the two dirty rivers, the Sava and the Danube, have had much appeal. They filled him no doubt with a deep corroding nostalgia for the open sea and The Men Who Go Down To It In Ships. This might explain the sudden brainstorm which overpowered him when he saw the entire Diplomatic Corps afloat on the Sava. Human motives are dark and obscure. I find it hard in my heart to judge Benbow."

"When was all this?"

"The year after you were posted."

Antrobus waved his cigar and settled himself more deeply in his favourite arm-chair. "It was a slack period diplomatically and as always happens during slack periods the Corps busied itself in trying to see which Mission could give the most original parties. The Americans gave an ill-judged moonlight bathing party on the island of Spam during which the Corps swam as one man into a field of jellyfish and a special plane had to be chartered to bring medical supplies to those who were stung. Then the Italians, not to be outdone, gave a party in a ruined monastery surrounded with cherry orchards—a picturesque enough choice of *venue*. But the season was well advanced and they had entirely failed to take into account the Greater Panslav Mosquito—an entomological curiosity to be reckoned with. It is the only animal I know which can bite effortlessly through trousers and under-pants all in one flowing movement. We all came back to Belgrade terribly swollen up and all different shapes and sizes. Then the Finns gave a concert of Serbian folk-music to which the band turned up drunk. Finally it seemed to Polk-Mowbray that it was our turn to be creative and a chit was passed down asking for ideas.

"I think it was De Mandeville who suggested a river party. Certainly it was not Benbow's idea; he had been very subdued that winter and apart from confessing that he was clairvoyant at parties and dabbling in astrology he had lived an exemplary life of restraint.

"Nor, on the face of it, was the idea a bad one. All winter long the logs come down the River Sava until the frost locks them in; with the spring thaw the east bank of the river has a pontoon of tree-trunks some forty feet wide lining the bank under the willows so that you can walk out over the river, avoiding the muddy margins, and swim in the deep water. The logs themselves are lightly tacked together with stapled wire by the lumber-jacks and they stay there till the autumn when they are untacked again and given a push into mid-stream. They then float on down to the sawmills. Here, as you know, the diplomatic corps swims all summer long. Though the muddy banks of the stream are infested with mosquitoes the light river wind ten yards from the shore creates a free zone. And jolly pleasant it is, as you probably remember.

"Well, this was the site selected for a river party by candle-light—the summer nights are breathlessly still—and Polk-Mowbray threw himself into the arrangements with great abandon. First of all he made sure that over the selected area the logs were really tacked firmly together. An immense tarpaulin was then spread and nailed down.

This made a raft about a hundred feet by sixty—big enough even to dance on. The Sava water cushioned the thing perfectly. A light marquee was run up and a long series of trestles to take a buffet. It promised to be the most original party of the year—and I'm not sure in retrospect whether it wasn't the most original I have ever attended. De Mandeville and his chauffeur were in the seventh heaven of delight; they organized a wickerwork fence round the raft with little gates leading to the dance floor and so on. There was also a changing-room for those who might decide to stay on and bathe. All in all it was most creditable to those concerned.

"The Corps itself was in ecstasies as it climbed the brightly painted gangplank on to the raft with its gaily lit buffet and striped marquee. Everyone turned up in full splendour and Polk-Mowbray himself made what he called his Special Effort: the cuff-links given to him by King Paul of Greece, the studs given to him by Queen Marie of Rumania, the cigarette-case by De Gaulle, and the cigar-cutter by Churchill. Darkness and candlelight and the buzz of Diplomatic exchanging Views was offset by the soft strains of Bozo's Gypsy Quartet which played sagging Serbian melodies full of glissandos and vibratos and long slimy arpeggios. It was an enchanting scene. The Press Corps was represented by poor Tope (Neuter's Special Correspondent) who was rapidly transported into nirvana by the awfully good Bollinger.

"You will ask yourself how the thing could possibly have gone wrong—and I cannot answer you for certain. All I know is that out of the corner of my eye I think I caught sight of a figure—was it Benbow?—sneaking furtively among the willows on the bank with what seemed to be a hatchet in his hand. More I cannot say.

"But I can be definite about one thing; while everyone was dancing the rumba and while the buffet was plying a heavy trade, it was noticed that the distance between the raft and the shore had sensibly increased. The gangplank subsided in the ooze. It was not a great distance—perhaps ten feet. But owing to the solid resistance such a large raft set up in the main current the pull was definitely outward. But as yet nobody was alarmed; indeed most of the members of the Corps thought it was part of a planned entertainment. I suppose most of the passengers on the *Titanic* turned in the night before the iceberg with just the same comfortable sense of well-being.

"Polk-Mowbray himself was concerned, it is true, though he did not lose composure. 'Can't some of you secretaries get out and push it back to the bank?' he asked; but the water was already too deep. For a long minute the lighted raft hung like a water-fly on the smooth surface of the river and then slowly began to move downstream in the calm night air, the candles fluttering softly, the band playing, and the Corps dancing or smoking or gossiping, thoroughly at peace with itself. There was at this stage some hope that at the next bend of the river the whole thing would run aground on the bank, and a few of us made preparations to grab hold of the log pontoons or the overhanging willows and halt our progress. But by ill luck an eddy carried us just too far into the centre of the river and we were carried past the spit of land, vainly groping at the tips of bushes.

"By now our situation deserved serious thought. There was literally no stop now until we reached Belgrade and here—the sweat started out on me as I thought of it—the Danube joins the Sava and causes something like a tidal bore, a permanent whirlpool. While the Sava is comparatively sluggish the Danube comes down from Rumania at about fourteen knots—impossible to swim in or ford. The point of junction is just below the fortress of Belgrade, a picturesque enough spot for those on dry land. . . .

"It was about five minutes before the full significance of our position began to dawn upon the Corps and by this time we were moving in stately fashion down the centre of the fairway, all lit up like a Christmas tree. Expostulations, suggestions, counter-suggestions poured from the lips of the diplomats and their wives in a dozen tongues.

"Unknown to us, too, other factors were being introduced which were to make this a memorable night for us all. Yugoslavia, as you know, was hemmed in at this time by extremely angry Communist states which kept her in a perpetual state of alarm by moving troops about on her borders, or by floating recriminatory and sometimes pornographic literature down the rivers which intersected the country—in an attempt, one imagines, to unman Serbian Womanhood, if such a thing be possible. At any rate, spy-mania was at meridian and the Yugoslav forces lived in a permanent state of alertness. There were frequent rumours of armed incursions from Hungary and Czechoslovakia. . . .

"It was in this context that some wretched Serbian infantryman at an observation post along the river saw what he took to be a large armed man-of-war full of Czech paratroops in dinner jackets and ball-dresses sailing upon Belgrade, the capital. He did not wait to verify this first impression. Glaucous-eyed, he galloped into Belgrade castle a quarter of an hour later on a foam-flecked mule with the news that the city was about to be invested.

The tocsin was sounded, while we, blissfully unaware of this, sailed softly down the dark water to our doom.

"It was lucky that there was only one gun in Belgrade castle. This was manned by Comrade Popovic and a scratch team of Albanian Shiptars clad in skull caps of white wool and goatskin breeches. (Fearsome to look at because of his huge moustache and shapeless physique the Shiptar is really a peaceable animal, about as quarrelsome as a Labrador and with the personality of a goldfish.) Usually it took the team about a week to load the Gun, which was a relic left behind them by the departing Visigoths or Ostrogoths—I forget which. Strictly speaking, too, it was not an offensive weapon as such but a Saluting Gun. Every evening during Ramadan it would give a hoarse boom at sunset, while a pair of blue underpants, which had been used from time immemorial as wadding for the blank charge, would stiffen themselves out on the sky.

"Nevertheless, when the news of the invasion reached Comrade Popovic he realized in a flash that the defence of the city depended entirely on him. He closed his eyes for a brief moment and saw himself receiving, in rapid succession, the Order of the Sava, The Order of St. Michael First Class, the Order of Mercy and Plenty with crossed Haystacks, and the Titotalitarian Medal of Honour with froggings. He set his platoon the task of scraping together a lethal charge capable of scattering the invaders as they came round the bend in the river. This was to be composed of a heterogeneous collection of beer bottle tops, discarded trouser buttons, cigarette-tins and fragments of discarded railway train. The aged gun was slewed round after a violent spell of man-hauling and brought to bear upon the target area.

"Meanwhile things aboard the raft were not going too well. Signs of incipient disintegration had begun to set in. Some of De Mandeville's artful trellis work had gone while the whole buffet had rather surprisingly broken off from the main body and started on a journey of its own down a narrow tributary of the river. I still remember the frozen faces of the waiters as they gazed around them despairingly like penguins on an ice-floe. Bozo's Band still kept up a pitiful simulacrum of sound but they had to keep moving position as the water was leaking along the tarpaulin and enveloping their ankles. Many of the candles had gone out. The chill of despair had begun to settle on the faces of the diplomats as the full urgency of the situation became plain to them. In their mind's eye they could hear—not to mix a metaphor—the fateful roar of the Danube water in its collision with the slow and peaceful Sava. Involuntary exclamations burst from the more voluble ladies. Was there nothing we could do? Could we not signal? Perhaps if we lit a fire . . . ? But these were counsels of despair as well they knew. I think we all felt in our bones that we should have to swim for it. The Italian Ambassador who had not swum for a quarter of a century tried a few tentative strokes in the air in a vain attempt to remember the routine. The only lucky person was Tope who had fallen asleep under the bar and was being borne off steadily down the tributary towards the sawmills where presumably he would be cut up by absent-minded Serbs and turned into newsprint— a fitting end.

"By this time we had reached the fatal bend in the river overlooked by the bastions of the castle where Pithecan- thropos Popovic waited, eyes on the river, safety match at the ready. The Gun was loaded to the brim. He knew he could not afford to miss us as it would be at least a week before the raw material for another lethal charge could be gathered from the dustbins of Belgrade. It was now or never. He drew a deep ecstatic breath as he saw us come round the bend, slowly, fatefully, straight into his line of fire. He applied the safety match to the touch-hole.

"There was a husky roar and the night above us was torn by a lurid yellow flash while the still water round the raft was suddenly ripped and pock-marked by a hail of what seemed to us pretty sizeable chain-shot. Pandemonium broke out. 'My God,' cried the Argentine Minister, who always showed a larger White Feather than anyone else, 'they're shooting at us!' He took refuge behind the massive Hanoverian frame of Madame Hess, wife of the German First Secretary. 'Throw yourselves on your faces!' cried the Swiss Minister, suiting the action to the word. The Italian Ambassador refused this injunction with some hauteur. 'Porca Madonna, I shall die standing up,' he cried, striking an attitude with one hand on his breast.

"Though nobody was actually hurt the bombardment had carried away most of the band's instruments, half the marquee and the rest of the De Mandeville's dainty trellis-work. It had also holed an ice-box filled with tomato juice and scattered the stuff, with its fearful resemblance to blood, all over us, so that many of us looked cut to pieces. Nor did we know then that it would take Comrade Popovic a week to repeat his exploit. We expected a dozen more guns to open on us as we neared the city. Some of the ladies began to cry, and others to staunch the apparent wounds made by the flying tomato juice on their menfolk. The Argentine Minister, suddenly noticing a red stain spreading on his white dinner-jacket front cried out: 'Caramba! They've got me!' and fell in a dead faint at Madame Hess's feet.

"The raft looked like a Victorian battle-piece by a master of anecdote. Some lay on their faces, some crouched behind chairs, some stood gesticulating, but all were racked with moans. It was now, too, that Polk-Mowbray turned savagely on poor De Mandeville and hissed: 'Why don't you do something? Why don't you shout for help?' Obediently above the racket De Mandeville raised his pitiful female-impersonator's screams: 'Help! Help!' into the enigmatic night.

"No further guns barked at us from the fort but by now the river had narrowed and its flow had increased. The raft began to spin round and round in a series of sickening rotations as it neared the fateful junction. Ahead of us we could see the blaze of searchlights and the stir of river traffic. My God, what fresh trials were awaiting us down there at the whirlpool's edge? Perhaps squads of whiskered Serbs were waiting to greet us with a hail of small-arms fire. A green-and-red rocket shot up in the farther darkness, increasing our alarm.

"Now the only people who had been of any real assistance to us in our predicament (though we did not know it then) were the chauffeurs of the Diplomatic Corps. They were mostly Serbian and virtually constituted a Corps on their own; jutting foreheads, lowering forelocks, buck teeth, webbed hands and feet, vast outcrops of untamed hair stretching away to every skyline. . . . They alone had watched our departure with alarm—with shrill ululations and inarticulate cries as they shifted their feet about in the ooze and watched the raft borne to its destruction. Moreover, they remembered what happened at the confluence of the two rivers. No sooner, therefore,

were we out of sight than the chauffeurs started out for town—a long gleaming line of official limousines.

"They had the sense, moreover, to go down to the dock and alert the river police and to enlist the aid of all the inhabitants of the coal quay whose bum-boats might be of use in grounding the raft before it reached the Niagara Falls. Two police boats with searchlights and a variety of sweat-stained small-boat owners accordingly set off up the Sava to head us off. This was the meaning of the lights and rockets on the river which caused us so much alarm.

"But they had reckoned without the mean size of the raft; even with all the missing bits which had flaked off it was still the size of a ballroom floor and correspondingly heavy. The bum-boats and the river launches met us in sickening collision about four hundred yards above the river junction. We were by this time so confused and shaken as to be almost out of our minds. Most of us thought that we had been attacked by pirates, and this impression was heightened when a huge Serb picked up Madame Hess in one hand and deposited her in his bum-boat. Cries of 'Rape!' went up from the Latin-American secretaries who had seen this sort of thing before. Meanwhile, half-blinded by searchlights and repeatedly knocked off their feet by the concussion of launches hitting the raft, the Swedish Embassy, in one of those sudden attacks of hysteria which afflict Nordics, decided to die to the last man rather than allow our rescuers aboard. The friendly, willing Serbs suddenly found themselves grappled by lithe young men clad in dinner jackets who sank their teeth into their necks and rolled overboard with them. A disgraceful *fracas* ensued. Despite the powerful engines of the river launches, too, the raft was irresistibly moving towards the rapids carrying not only the Flower of European Diplomacy but also a large assortment of bum-boats whose owners were letting out shrill cries and rowing in every direction but the right one.

"It was all over with us, old man. Not exactly in a flash but in a series of movements like a bucking bronco. Those of us who had read Conrad's *Typhoon* felt we had been here before.

"The Danube ripped the tarpaulin off, unstapled the logs and threw everything into the air. It was lucky that there were enough logs to go round. I can't say the Diplomatic Corps looked its best sitting astride logs with the water foaming round it, but it was certainly something you don't see every day. The Argentine Minister was borne screaming off into the night and only picked up next morning ten miles down river. Indeed, the banks of the Danube as far as the town of Smog were littered with the whitening bones of Swedes and Finns and Japs and Greeks. De Mandeville was struck on the head and knocked insensible; Polk-Mowbray broke his collar bone. Draper lost a toupee which cost about a hundred pounds and was forced to go about in a beret for nearly two months.

"We could not call the roll for twenty-four hours and when we did it seemed nothing less than a miracle that we had endured no major casualties. It's the sort of thing which almost makes one Take Refuge in Religion.

"As for Benbow, he had gone on long leave by next morning and was not due back for six months. It was a tactful retreat. Polk-Mowbray himself drew the moral and adorned the tale by remarking to the Chancery: 'The Great Thing in Diplomacy is Never to Over-reach Oneself.' I think he had got hold of something there, even if he was just being wise after the event."

10

La Valise

"If there is anything worse than a soprano," said Antrobus judicially as we walked down the Mall towards his club, "it is a mezzo-soprano. One shriek lower in the scale, perhaps, but with higher candle-power. I'm not just being small-minded, old chap. I bear the scars of spiritual experience. Seriously." And indeed he did look serious; but then he always does. The aura of the Foreign Office clings to him. He waved his umbrella, changed step, and continued in a lower, more confidential register. "And I can tell you another thing. If there is anything really questionable about the French character it must be its passion for *culture*. I might not dare to say this in the F.O. old man, but I know you will respect my confidence. You see, we are all supposed to be pro rather than anti in the Old Firm—but as for me, frankly I hate the stuff. It rattles me. It gives me the plain untitivated pip, I don't mind confessing."

He drew a deep breath and after a pause went on,

more pensively, drawing upon his memories of Foreign Service life: "All my worst moments have been cultural rather than political. Like that awful business of *La Valise*, known privately to the members of the Corps as The Diplomatic Bag Extraordinary. Did I ever mention it? She was French Ambassadress in Poland."

"No."

"Shall I? It will make you wince."

"Do."

"Well it happened while I was serving in Warsaw some years ago; an unspeakable place full of unspeakable people. It was the usual Iron Curtain post to which the F.O. had exposed its soft white underbelly in the person of Smith-Cromwell. Not that he was a bad chap. He was in fact quite intelligent and had played darts for Cambridge. But he was easily led. As you know in a Communist country the Corps finds itself cut off from every human contact. It has to provide its own amusements, fall back on its own resources. And this is where the trouble usually begins. It is a strange thing, but in a post like that it is never long before some dastardly Frenchman (always French) reaches for the safety catch of his revolver and starts to introduce *culture* into our lives. Invariably.

"So it fell out with us in Warsaw. Sure enough, during my second winter the French appointed a Cultural Attaché, straight from Montmartre—the place with the big church. Fellow like a greyhound. Burning eyes. Dirty hair. A moist and Fahrenheit handshake. You know the type. Started living quite openly with a girl in the secret police. Most Questionable fellow. Up till now everything had been quiet and

91

reasonable—just the usual round of diplomatic-social engagements among colleagues. Now this beastly fellow started the ball rolling with a public lecture—an undisguised public lecture—on a French writer called, if I understood him correctly, Flowbear. Of course we all had to go to support the French. Cultural reciprocity and all that. But as if this wasn't enough, the little blackhead followed it up with another about another blasted French writer called, unless my memory is at fault, Goaty-eh. I ask you, my dear fellow, what was one to do. Flowbear! Goaty-eh! It was more than flesh and blood could stand. I myself feared the worst as I sat listening to him. I had of course wound up and set my features at Refined Rapture like everyone else, but inside me I was in a turmoil of apprehension. Culture spreads like mumps, you know, like measles. A thing like this could get everyone acting unnaturally in no time. All culture corrupts, old boy, but French culture corrupts absolutely. I was not wrong.

"The echoes had hardly died away when I noticed That awful look coming over people's faces. Everyone began to think up little tortures of their own. A whole winter stretched before us with practically no engagements except a national day or so. It was clear that unless Smith-Cromwell took a strong line the rot would set in. He did not. Instead of snorting when La Valise embarked on a cultural season he weakly encouraged her; he was even heard to remark that culture was a Good Thing—for the Military Attaché.

"At this time of course we also had our cultural man. Name of Gool. And he looked it. It was a clear case of Harrow and a bad third in History. But up to now we had kept Gool strictly under control and afraid to move. It could not last. He was bound to come adrift. Within a month he was making common cause with his French colleague. They began to lecture, separately and together. They gave readings with writhings. They spared us nothing, Eliot, Sartre, Immanuel Kant—and who is that other fellow? The name escapes me. In short they gave us everything short of Mrs. Beeton. I did my best to get an arm-lock on Gool and to a certain extent succeeded by threatening to recommend him for an OBE. He knew this would ruin his career and that he would be posted to Java. But by the time I had got him pressed to the mat it was too late. The whole Corps had taken fire and was burning with the old hard gem-like flame. Culture was spreading like wildfire.

"A series of unforgettable evenings now began, old boy. Each mission thought up some particularly horrible contribution of its own to this feast. The nights became a torture of pure poesy and song. An evening of hellish amateur opera by the Italians would be followed without intermission by an ear-splitting evening of yodelling from the Swiss, all dressed as edelweiss. Then the Japanese mission went berserk and gave a Noh-play of ghoulish obscurity lasting seven hours. The sight of all those little yellowish, inscrutable diplomats all dressed as Mickey Mouse, old boy, was enough to turn milk. And their voices simply ate into one. Then in characteristic fashion the Dutch, not to be outdone, decided to gnaw their way to the forefront of things with a recital of national poetry by the Dutch Ambassadress herself. This was when I began to draft my resignation in my own mind. O

93

God! how can I ever forget Madame Vanderpipf (usually the most kind and normal of wives and mothers) taking up a stance like a grenadier at Fontenoy, and after a pause declaiming in a slow, deep—O unspeakably slow and deep—voice, the opening verses of whatever it was? Old boy, the cultural heritage of the Dutch is not my affair. Let them have it, I say. Let them enjoy it peacefully as they may. But spare me from poems of five hundred lines beginning '*Oom kroop der poop.*' You smile, as well indeed you may, never having heard Mrs. Vanderpipf declaiming those memorable stanzas with all the sullen fire of her race. Listen!

> *Oom kroop der poop*
> *Zoom kroon der soup*
> *Soon droon der oopersnoop.*

"And so on. Have you got the idea? Perhaps there is something behind it all—who am I to say? All I know is that it is no joke to be on the receiving end. Specially as she would pause from time to time to give a rough translation in pidgin for Smith-Cromwell's benefit. Something like this: 'Our national poet Snugerpouf, he says, eef Holland lives forever, only, how you would say? heroes from ze soil oospringing, yes?'

"Then she would take a deep breath and begin afresh.

> *Oom kroop der poop*
> *Zoom kroon der soup.*

"In after years the very memory of this recitation used to make the sweat start out on my forehead. You must try it for yourself sometime. Just try repeating '*oom kroop der poop*' five hundred times in a low voice.

LA VALISE

After a time it's like Yoga. Everything goes dark. You feel you are falling back into illimitable space.

"By this time Smith-Cromwell himself had begun to suffer. He leaned across to me once on this particular evening to whisper a message. I could tell from his popping eye and the knot of throbbing veins at his temple that he was under strain. He had at last discovered what culture means. 'If this goes on much longer,' he hissed, 'I shall confess everything.'

"But this did go on; unremittingly for a whole winter. I spare you a description of the cultural offerings brought to us by the remoter tribes. The Argentines! The Liberians! Dear God! When I think of the Chinese all dressed in lampshades, the Australians doing sheep-opera, the Egyptians undulating and ululating all in the same breath. . . . Old boy, I am at a loss.

"But the real evil demon of the piece was *La Valise*. Whenever culture flagged she was there, quick to rekindle the flame. Long after the Corps was milked dry, so to speak, and had nothing left in its collective memory except nursery rhymes or perhaps a dirty limerick or two, *La Valise* was still at it. She fancied herself as a singer. She was never without a wad of music. A mezzo-soprano never gives in, old boy. She dies standing up, with swelling port curved to the stars. . . . And here came this beastly attaché again. He had turned out to be a pianist, and she took him everywhere to accompany her. While he clawed the piano she clawed the air and remorselessly sang. How she sang! Always a bit flat, I gather, but with a sickening lucid resonance that penetrated the inner ear. Those who had hearing-aids filled them with a kapok mixture for her recitals. When she hit a top note I could hear the studs vibrating in my dinner-shirt. Cowed, we sat and watched her, as she started to climb a row of notes towards the veil of the temple— that shattering top E, F, or G: I never know which. We had the sinking feeling you get on the giant racer just as it nears the top of the slope. To this day I don't know how we kept our heads.

"Smith-Cromwell was by this time deeply penitent about his earlier encouragement of *La Valise* and at his wits' end to see her stopped. Everyone in the Chancery was in a bad state of nerves. The Naval Attaché had taken to bursting into tears at meals if one so much as mentioned a forthcoming cultural engagement. But what was to be done? We clutched at every straw; and De Mandeville, always resourceful, suggesting inviting the Corps to a live reading by himself and chauffeur from the works of the Marquis de Sade. But after deliberation Smith-Cromwell thought this might, though effective, seem Questionable, so we dropped it.

"I had begun to feel like Titus Andronicus, old man, when the miracle happened. Out of a cloudless sky. Nemesis intervened just as he does in Gilbert Murray. Now *La Valise* had always been somewhat hirsute, indeed quite distinctly moustached in the Neapolitan manner, though none of us for a moment suspected the truth. But one day after Christmas M. De Panier, her husband, came round to the Embassy in full *tenu* and threw himself into Cromwell-Smith's arms, bathed in tears as the French always say. 'My dear Britannic Colleague,' he said, 'I have come to take my leave of you. My career is completely ruined. I am leaving

Vasiliu

diplomacy for good. I have resigned. I shall return to my father-in-law's carpet-factory near Lyons and start a new life. All is over.'

"Smith-Cromwell was of course delighted to see the back of *La Valise;* but we all had a soft corner for De Panier. He was a gentleman. Never scamped his *frais* and always gave us real champagne on Bastille Day. Also his dinners were dinners—not like the Swedes'; but I am straying from my point. In answer to Smith-Cromwell's tactful enquiries De Panier unbosomed.

"You will never credit it, old man. You will think I am romancing. But it's as true as I am standing here. There are times in life when the heart spires upward like the lark on the wing; when through the consciousness runs, like an unearthly melody, the thought that God *really* exists, really *cares;* more, that he turns aside to lend a helping hand to poor dips *in extremis.* This was such a moment, old boy.

"*La Valise* had gone into hospital for some minor complaint which defied diagnosis. And in the course of a minor operation the doctors discovered that she was *turning into a man!* Nowadays, of course, it is becoming a commonplace of medicine; but at the time of which I speak it sounded like a miracle. A *man,* upon my soul! We could hardly believe it. The old caterpillar was really one of *us.* It was too enchanting! We were saved!

"And so it turned out. Within a matter of months her voice—that instrument of stark doom—sank to a bass; she sprouted a beard. Poor old De Panier hastened to leave but was held up until his replacement came. Poor fellow! Our hearts went out to him with this Whiskered Wonder on his hands. But he took it all very gallantly. They left at last, in a closed car, at dead of night. He would be happier in Lyons, I reflected, where nobody minds that sort of thing.

"But if he was gallant about this misfortune so was *La Valise elle-même*. She went on the halls, old boy, as a bass baritone and made quite a name for herself. Smith-Cromwell says he once heard her sing 'The London Derriere' in Paris with full orchestra and that she brought the house down. Some of the lower notes still made the ash-trays vibrate a bit but it was no longer like being trapped in a wind-tunnel. She wore a beard now and a corkscrew moustache and was very self-possessed. One can afford to be in France. He also noticed she was wearing a smartish pair of elastic-sided boots. O, and her trade name now was Tito Torez. She and De Panier were divorced by then, and she had started out on a new career which was less of a reign of terror, if we can trust Smith-Cromwell. Merciful are the ways of Providence!

"As for poor De Panier himself, I gather that he re-entered the service after the scandal had died down. He is at present Consul General in Denver, Colorado. I'm told that there isn't much culture there, so he ought to be a very happy man."

11

Cry Wolf

"The case of Wormwood," said Antrobus gravely, "is one which deserves thought."

He spoke in his usual portentous way, but I could see that he was genuinely troubled.

"It is worth reflecting on," he went on, "since it illustrates my contention that nobody really knows what anybody else is thinking. Wormwood was Cultural Attache in Helsinki, and we were all terrified of him. He was a lean, leathery, saturnine sort of chap with a goatee and he'd written a couple of novels of an obscurity so overwhelming as to give us an awful inferiority complex in the Chancery.

"He never spoke.

"He carried this utter speechlessness to such lengths as to be almost beyond the bounds of decency. The whole Corps quailed before him. One slow stare through those pebble-giglamps of his was enough to quell even the vivid and charming Madam Abreyville who was noted for her cleverness in bringing out the

Vasiliu

shy. She made the mistake of trying to bring Worm-wood out. He stared at her hard. She was covered in confusion and trembled from head to foot. After this defeat, we all used to take cover when we saw him coming.

"One winter, just before he was posted to Prague, I ran into him at a party, and finding myself wedged in behind the piano with no hope of escape, cleared my throat (I had had three Martinis) and said with what I hoped was offensive jocularity: 'What does a novelist think about at parties like these?'

"Wormwood stared at me for so long that I began to swallow my Adam's apple over and over again as I always do when I am out of countenance. I was just about to step out of the window into a flower bed and come round by the front door when he . . . actually spoke to me: 'Do you know what I am doing?' he said in a low hissing tone full of malevolence.

" 'No,' I said.

" 'I am playing a little game in my mind,' he said, and his expression was one of utter, murderous grim-ness. 'I am imagining that I am in a sleigh with the whole Diplomatic Corps. We are rushing across the steppes, pursued by wolves. It is necessary, as they keep gaining on us, to throw a diplomat overboard from time to time in order to let the horses regain their advantage. Who would you throw first . . . and then second . . . and then third . . . ? Just look around you.'

"His tone was so alarming, so ferocious and per-emptory, that I was startled; more to humour him than anything else, I said 'Madame Ventura.' She was rather a heavily-built morsel of ambassadress, eminently suitable for wolfish consumption. He curled his lip. 'She's gone already,' he said in a low, hoarse tone, glowering. 'The whole Italian mission has gone—brats included.'

"I did not quite know what to say.

"'Er, how about our own Chancery?' I asked nervously.

"'Oh! They've gone long ago,' he said with slow contempt, 'They've been gobbled up—including you.' He gave a yellowish shelf of rat-like teeth a half-second exposure, and then sheathed them again in his beard. I was feeling dashed awkard now, and found myself fingering my nose.

"I was relieved when I heard he had been posted.

"Now, old boy, comes a series of strange events. The very next winter in Prague—that was the severe one of '37 when the wolf packs came down to the suburbs—you may remember that two Chancery guards and a cipher clerk were eaten by wolves? They were, it seems, out riding in a sleigh with the First Secretary Cultural. When I saw the press reports, something seemed to ring in my brain. Some half-forgotten memory. . . . It worried me until I went to the Foreign Office List and looked up the Prague Mission. It was Wormwood. It gave me food for deep thought.

"But time passed, and for nearly ten years I heard no more of Wormwood. Then came that report of wolves eating the Italian Ambassador on the Trieste-Zagreb road in mid-winter. You remember the case? The victim was in a car this time. I do not have to tell you who was driving. Wormwood.

"Then once again a long period of time passed without any news of him. But yesterday . . ." Antrobus' voice trembled at this point in the narrative and he drew heavily on his cigar.

"Yesterday, I had a long letter from Bunty Scott-Peverel who is Head of Chancery in Moscow. There is a passage in it which I will read to you. Here it is. . . .

" 'We have just got a new Cultural Sec., rather an odd sort of fellow, a writer I believe. Huge fronded beard, pebble specs, and glum as all highbrows are. He has taken a *dumka* about twenty miles outside Moscow where he intends to entertain in some style. Usually these hunting lodges are only open in the summer. But he intends to travel by *droshky* and is busy getting one built big enough, he says, to accommodate the whole Dip. Corps, which he will invite to his housewarming. It is rather an original idea, and we are all looking forward to it very much and waiting impatiently for this giant among *droshkies* to be finished.'

"You will understand," said Antrobus, "the thrill of horror with which I read this letter. I have written at length to Bunty, setting out my fears. I hope I shall be in time to avert what might easily become the first wholesale pogrom in the history of diplomacy. I hope he heeds my words. But I am worried, I confess. I scan the papers uneasily every morning. Is that the *Telegraph*, by any chance, protruding from the pocket of your mackintosh?"

Stiff Upper Lip

To
RICHARD ALDINGTON
who encouraged these follies

Contents

Contents

Stiff Upper Lip

"Answer me at once, or in Heaven's name I'll———"

1

If Garlic be the Food of Love...

Every Wednesday now, in the winter, I lunch with
Antrobus at his club, picking him up at the Foreign
Office just before noon. I think he enjoys these meetings
as much as I do for they enable him to reminisce about
old times in the Foreign Service. For my part I am always
glad to add an anecdote or two to my private *Antrobus
File*—the groundwork upon which I one day hope to
raise the monument of my own Diplomatic Memories....

Yesterday his memory carried him back to Vulgaria
again where he had served under Polk-Mowbray—and
over De Mandeville—as Head of Chancery. "Bitter days,"
he mused. "And perhaps one shouldn't talk about them.
De Mandeville was in a queer state all that spring; perhaps
it had something to do with the phases of the moon? I
don't know. He was in a "Hamlet, Revenge!" sort of
mood. The trouble seemed to centre about the Embassy
table—as Third Sec. he had a watching brief on the food.
It started I remembered with a series of Constance Spry
table-decorations which made that otherwise fairly festive
board look like an illustration from the Jungle Books.

One could hardly carry a fork to one's mouth without biting off a piece of fern by mistake. Slices of decorative pumpkin and marrow gave a Harvest Festival note to things. One peered at one's guests through a forest of potted plants. Finally Polk-Mowbray put his foot down. De Mandeville became huffed. The next thing was he ordered Drage to serve everything from the right—in deference to a left-handed Trade Mission chief who was staying with us. It may have been tactful but it led to endless complications with us right-handed trenchermen who found everything upside down, and had to scuffle to rearrange our table-patterns as we sat down. And then what with Drage coming in so fast from the wrong side one was practically always out, hit-wicket on the *soufflé*. I tried to reason with De Mandeville but he only pouted and bridled. It was clear that he was in an ugly mood, old boy. I feared the worst. I have a sort of intuition about these things.

"The next thing in this chain of progressive sabotage was curry. De Mandeville had a series of Madras curries served. They were of such a blistering intensity that the entire Dutch Embassy had the inside of its collective mouth burned away—peeled off like bark from a tree, old boy. The Minister called on Polk-Mowbray in *tenue* and wanted to know if a state of war existed between England and Holland. His wife had to be treated for soft palate. A junior attaché went about saying that the Embassy food was full of quicklime and hinting darkly about damages. Naturally there were high words and massive contempts flying about which made Polk-Mowbray somewhat nervy. De Mandeville was sharply taken to task, but without avail. He next served an onion soup and black bread without soup-spoons. You know how long a rich onion

IF GARLIC BE THE FOOD OF LOVE . . .

soup takes to cool. Our little lunch-party dragged on almost to dusk, and several guests were lightly scalded because they neglected to take thermometer readings before gulping. The whole thing was gradually working up towards a climax. I saw it all coming and mentally, so to speak, closed my eyes and breathed a prayer to the Goddess of Diplomacy. I could not, however, guess from which quarter this warped and twisted Third Sec. might deliver the knock-out blow.

"Then . . . all this is in the strictest confidence, old man. . . . Then it came. Polk-Mowbray used to leave his office door wide open so I could see and hear all that went on therein. One morning I heard a familiar sort of row going on and I knew that the blow had fallen at last. Polk-Mowbray was hysterical. 'I adjure you by the bones of Cromer', he was yelling, 'to answer me without prevarication. *Have you been putting garlic in the food without telling anyone?* Did you, wittingly or unwittingly plug that *cassoulet*, impregnate that lustreless salad, order the peas to be lightly simmered in the stuff before serving? Answer me at once, or in Heaven's Name I'll——'

"De Mandeville made a gobbling self-deprecating sort of sound and spread his manicured hands as he muttered something about garlic being eaten in all the best London houses. It toned up the nervous system. Some said it was the only specific for scabies. One would have to be very retrograde to imagine. . . . And so on in this style. Veins were throbbing all over poor Polk-Mowbray by this time. 'Do not try to justify yourself,' he thundered. 'Answer me with a simple yea or nea. And take that beastly sensual smile off your face. If you choose to dine on heads of raw garlic with your scabrous chauffeur it is your business. But the Embassy table is sacred, do you

13

hear? *Sacred*. If you do not answer truthfully I shall make
you the subject of a General Paper to the Foreign Secretary.' There was a short silence during which they glared
at each other. Then De Mandeville threw back his chin
and uttered the word 'yes' rather defiantly; he was wearing an obstinate Canine Defence League expression on
his face. Polk-Mowbray levitated briefly and banged his
desk with a triumphant. 'Aha! So you *did*.' It was clear
that De Mandeville was in for one of those Searching Re-
proofs. His Chief now began to walk up and down his
own carpet as he always did when he was moved. He
Pointed The Finger Of Scorn at De Mandeville in no un-
certain fashion. 'Wretch!' he cried in a shaking voice.
'Could you not see the harm that might come from such
reckless and criminal cookery? Moreover you choose the
one lunch party of the year which is of policy importance
in order to do me the greatest damage. Think of the
Naval Attaché! What has he ever done to merit that unspeakable lunch—at which he ate far too heartily? And
my niece Angela—what of her? And the Head of the
Foreign Ministry—what of him?'

"De Mandeville tried to make a few unavailing pro-
tests. 'Enough!' cried Polk-Mowbray hoarsely. 'Surely
you know that to feed a Naval Attaché garlic is like
stoking a coke furnace with dead rats? Did you see his
face as he lurched out into the afternoon? You did not
know, I suppose, that he was due to lecture to the Sea
Wolves on Temperance and Self-Denial at sea? He
created a very poor impression in a very short time. The
wretch now fears court-martial. He says that now whenever his pinnace is sighted they raise a Yellow Fever flag
and forbid him access to the ship. I do not doubt that the
dirk-point will be facing him when he walks into the

ward-room. All this is on your head and more. Don't interrupt me. That is not all. Do you realize that when I helped the Minister into his car he was making a noise like a bunsen burner? *You* would not care that he had to address the High Praesidium that afternoon on Foreign Affairs—moreover in a language so full of aspirates as to make the gravest demands on his audience! No, *you* would not care, with your pumpkins and pottery and left-handed table arrangements! On you go in your headlong career, weaving these devilish plots around my table. And apart from all this what about *me*. *You* cannot be expected to know that I was booked to read the Lesson at a Memorial Service in the British Baptist Chapel which is notoriously cramped and ill-ventilated. How did you think I felt when I saw the first two rows of the congregation swaying like ripened wheat in an east wind? How do you think I felt when it came to my turn to embrace the hapless widow? She was breathing as if she had slipped her fan-belt. Answer me! You see, you haven't a word to say. You are mumchance as you jolly well ought to be. Fie on you, Aubrey de Mandeville! *You* did not stop to think what effect Angela might have on Cosgrave after such a lunch. The engagement was pretty tremulous as it was— but you snookered the wretched girl well and truly. And what of the typists' pool? Girls keeling over one after another as they tried to take dictation from us. What of them?' For a moment words failed him. His face worked. Then he said in a low murderous tone, from between clenched teeth. 'I tell you that from now on there is to be no more garlic. Sage, yes. Thyme, yes. Rosemary, marjoram, dill, cummin, yes. Emphatically yes. But *garlic*, no!' And so the edict went forth and the sale of peppermints in the Naafi dropped off again."

IF GARLIC BE THE FOOD OF LOVE . . .

Antrobus sighed sadly over these memories as he replenished our glasses. Then he said musingly: "I should say really that Garlic was the biggest Single Cross a Diplomat had to bear in the rough old times. It *had* to be banned, old man. Yet in a sense we were all Living A Lie, like the Americans under Prohibition; for we all secretly yearned after the stuff. (I say this in the strictest confidence. I would not wish to be quoted.) Yet it is strange that this noxious bulb should have such an allure for men. As for diplomats, it played havoc with Confidential Exchanges; and as for dancing with your Ambassadress . . .well. It was the quickest way to get posted. That is why I was so relieved when the Age Of Science dawned. I used to be *against* Science once, and for the Humanities—I freely admit it. But when at last chlorophyl came in I was instantly won over. What a boon and a blessing to dips! What an over-riding sense of relief! Many a breach was healed that day between man and man. Even Polk-Mowbray in the end allowed the salad-bowl to be lightly rubbed with a couple of heads before serving. And I don't know whether you noticed the rather respectable little *ragoût* we have just been eating? Not bad for the Club, is it? But fear nothing! In my pocket lies a phial full of those little grey tablets which make human intercourse a rational, easy, unbuttoned sort of thing again. No more shrinking from pursed lips in The Office. We can hold our heads high once more! Let's drink a final little toast to the Goddess of the F.O. shall we? I give you Chlorophyl!"

. . . une petite splendeur

2

Stiff Upper Lip

As for the Fair Sex (said Antrobus), I am no expert, old
boy. I've always steered clear. Mind you, I've admired
through binoculars as one might admire a fine pair of
antlers. Nearest I ever came to being enmeshed was in the
Folies Bergères one night. Fortunately, Sidney Trampelvis
was there and got me out into the night air and fanned me
with his cape until my head cleared and I realized the Full
Enormity of what I'd done. Without realizing it, I had
proposed to a delightful little pair of antlers called Fifi and
was proposing to take her back to the Embassy and force
the Chaplain to gum us up together. Phew! I certainly
owe Sidney a debt. We positively galloped away from the
place in a horse-drawn contrivance with our opera hats
crushed like puff-pastry. Sidney, who was only visiting,
and who had also crossed the subliminal threshold and
proposed—dear God—to a contortionist; Sidney was
even paler than I. That night he dyed his hair green to
escape identification and crossed over to Dover on the
dusk packet—a bundle of nerves.

19

But Dovebasket in love was a strange sight. His sighs echoed through the Chancery. There were sonnets and triolets and things all over the backs of the War Office despatches. The little winged youth had certainly pinked him through the spencer. Yes, it was Angela, Polk-Mowbray's niece. I can't think why Polk-Mowbray didn't liquidate one or both of them. But then the Popular Verdict on *him* was that he needed stiffening. Yes, the stiffest thing about him was perhaps his upper lip. As for Dovebasket, I would have described him as an ensanguined poop. A spoon, my dear chap, a mere spoon. Yet love makes no distinctions. Afterwards he published a little book of his poems called *Love Songs of an Assistant Military Attaché* with a preface by Havelock Ellis. A rum book in sooth. I remember one refrain:

> *The moon gleams up there like a cuspidor*
> *Angela, Angela, what are we waiting for?*

You get the sort of stuff? Could lead directly to Nudism. It was clear from all this that he was terribly oversexed and I for one felt that he would end in Botany Bay or the Conservative Central Office or somewhere. You see, Angela wouldn't respond to the rowel at all. Not her. Press his suit as firmly as he might the wretched chap only got the tip-tilted nose in response. It was clear that she considered him as no more than a worm-powder. And here I must add that we had all been worried about Angela, for she had been showing signs of getting one of her famous crushes on the Russian Military Attaché— Serge, or Tweed, or something by name—a bloater to boot. But of course, the worst aspect of it all was that we weren't officially fraternizing at that time with The Other Bloc. Polk-Mowbray was worried about her security. He had been frightfully alarmed to overhear an idle conversation of hers with a Pole in which she gave away—without a moment's thought—the entire lay-out of Henley Regatta, every disposition, old boy. She even drew a map of the refreshment room. I know that Henley isn't Top Secret, but it might just as easily have been the dispositions of the Home Fleet. Such lightness of speech argued ill for the Mission. One simply did not know what she mightn't reveal in this way. . . . We were concerned, I might say, Quite Concerned.

Well, it so fell out that during this fruitless romance of Dovebasket's the Vulgarians invited us all to join them in pushing out the boat for the Wine Industry. They had always had a Wine Industry, mind you, but it had never been put on a proper basis before. So, very wisely, they had imported a trio of French experts and turned them loose among the bins. Within a matter of a couple of years, the whole thing had been reorganized, new cultures had been sorted out, and Vulgaria was now about to launch about twenty new wines upon the export market. Advance intelligence from old Baron Hisse la Juppe, the Military Attaché (who had practically lived down there while experiments were going on) suggested that something most promising had taken place. Vulgaria, he said (rather precariously) was on the point of exporting wines which would equal anything the French and Italians could do. . . . We were incredulous, of course, but were glad to assist in the send-off of the new wines. The whole Corps accepted the invitation to the *Vin d'Honneur* with alacrity.

The day dawned bright and fair, and it was a merry party of carefree dips who took the train north to the vineyards. The whole *vieillesse dorée* of diplomacy, old man.

In sparkling trim. For once, the whole thing was admirably worked out; we were carried in vine-wreathed carriages to the great main cellars of the place—more like a railway tunnel than anything, where warm candle-light glowed upon twinkling glasses and white linen; where the music of minstrels sounded among the banks of flowers. . . . I must say, I was transported by the beauty of the scene. There lay the banks of labelled bottles, snoozing softly upon the trestles with the candles shining upon their new names. Our hosts made speeches. We cheered. Then corks began to pop and the wine-tasting began. One of the French specialists led us round. He tried to get us to take the thing rather too professionally—you know, shuffling it about in the mouth, cocking the chin up to the ceiling and then spitting out into a kind of stone draining-board. Well as you know, one is trained to do most things in the F.O. But not to spit out good wine. No. We simply wouldn't demean ourselves by this niggardly shuffling and spitting out. We swallowed. I think you would have done the same in our place. What we were given to taste, we tasted. But we put the stuff away.

And what stuff, my dear boy. Everything that Hisse la Juppe had said proved true. What wines! Wines to set dimples in the cheeks of the soul. Some were little demure white wines, skirts lifted just above the knee, as it were. Others just showed an elbow or an ankle. Others were as the flash of a nymph's thigh in the bracken. Wines in sables, wines in mink! What an achievement for the French! Some of the range of reds struck out all the deep bass organ-notes of passions—in cultured souls like ours. It was ripping. We expanded. We beamed. Life seemed awfully jolly all of a sudden. We rained congratulations upon our hosts as we gradually wound along the great cellars, tasting and judging. What wines! I couldn't decide for myself, but after many trials fell upon a red wine with a very good nose. You see, we each had to pick one, as a free crate of it was to be given to each member of the Corps. Sort of Advertisement.

And as we went along the French specialist enchanted us by reading out from his card the descriptions of the wines which we were trying. What poetry! I must hand it to the French, though they tend to make me suspicious in lots of ways. There was one, for example, a sort of hock, which was described as *"au fruité parfait, mais présentant encore une légère pointe de verdeur nullement désagréable.* Another was described as *"séveux et bien charpenté".* And then there was a sort of Vulgarian Meursault which was *"parfait de noblesse et de finesse, une petite splendeur."* I must say, for a moment one almost succumbed to culture, old man. The stuff was damned good. Soon we were all as merry as tom-tits, and I even smiled by mistake at the Bulgarian Chargé. In fact everything would have gone off like a dream if Dovebasket hadn't cut up rough and sat deliberately on the air-conditioning.

Apparently in the middle of all this bonhomie the wretched youth crept up on Angela and breathed a winged word in her ear. It was the old fateful pattern. She turned on her heel and tossing up her little chin went over to the other corner where the crapulous Serge was swigging the least significant of the wines with much smacking of the lips. It was so obvious; Dovebasket was cut as if by a whiplash. A cry of fury broke from his lips to find that she preferred this revolting foreigner who had apparently been named after an inferior British export material; he banged his fist upon the nearest table and cried out, "If I cannot have her, nobody shall!" And all of a sudden made his way to the corner of the tunnel of love and sat down. He took a copy of Palgrave's Golden Brewery from his pocket—one of those anthologies with a monotonous-looking cover—and started to read in a huffy way. Sulks, old man, mortal sulks.

Well, we sighed and went on with our bibbing, unaware that the fellow was sitting upon our life-line, as it were. I have already said that he was mechanically-minded. Apparently he had noticed that the air-supply to the tunnel came through a sort of sprocket with a side-valve cut in a sort of gasket with a remote-control intake —how does one say these things? Anyway. Dovebasket placed his behind firmly on the air-screw, thus cutting off our oxygen supply from the outer world. It was all very well trying to suffocate his rival. But—and such is the power of passion—he was determined to suffocate the entire Corps.

Well, for ages nobody noticed anything. On we went from cask to cask, in ever-growing merriment, getting more and more courtly, with each swig. We thought that Dovebasket was just alone and palely loitering, that he would grow out of it. We didn't know that he was sitting on the very H_2SO_4 or H_2O (I never was much good at chemistry) which nourished human life in these regions. I had never thought much about air before. Apparently there is something quite essential about it. Nutritious as wine is, it cannot apparently sustain life unaided. Well, as I say, there we were unaware of the formaldehyde bubbles which were slowly crawling up the bloodstream, mounting to our brains. Suddenly I noticed that everyone seemed unwontedly hilarious, a rather ghastly sort of hilarity, mind you. Laughter, talk, music—it all seemed to have gone into a new focus.

A grimly bacchanalian note set in. I was vaguely aware that things were not as they should be but I couldn't quite put my finger on it. The first to go was Gool, the British Council man. He lay down quietly in a bed of roses and passed out, only pausing to observe that he could feel the flowers growing over him. We ignored him. The music had got rather ragged at the edges. People were drinking on rather desperately now and talking louder than ever. Somewhere in the heart of it all there was a Marked Discomfort. People seemed suddenly to have aged, bent up. You could begin to see how they would look at ninety if they lived that long. The chiefs of mission had gone an ashen colour. As if they had worn their expressions almost down to the lining. It is hardly believable what a difference air can make to dips, old man.

And now it was that knees began to buckle, stays to creak, guy-ropes to give. Still, in courtly fashion, people began to look around them for something to lean on. Yes, people everywhere began to strap-hang, still talking and laughing, but somehow in a precarious way. Polk-Mowbray had gone a distinctly chalky colour and had difficulty in articulating; the Argentine Minister had quite frankly started to crawl towards the entrance on all fours.

It was Serge, I think, who first noticed the cause of our plight. With a bound he was at Dovebasket's side crying, "Please to remove posterior from the breathing," in quite good Satellite English. Dovebasket declined to do so. Serge pulled him and received a knee in the chest. Dovebasket settled himself firmly once more and showed clearly that he wasn't letting any more air in that week. Serge seized a wicker-covered bottle of the Chianti type and tapped him smartly on the crown. Dovebasket was not going to be treated like a breakfast egg by his hated rival. He dotted him back. This was fatal. One could see at once how wars break out. Poland and Rumania came to the Assistance of Serge, while Canada and Australia answered the call of the Mother Country. It looked like some strange Saturnalia, armed dips circling each other with wicker-covered bottles.

But as the fighting spread, Dovebasket got shifted from his perch and the life-giving H_2SO_4 began to pour once more into the cave. It was only just in time, I should say. The cellar now looked like a series of whimsical details from a Victorian canvas—I'm thinking of "Kiss Me Hardy" with Nelson down for the count in the Victory's cockpit. Some were kneeling in pleading postures. Some were crawling about in that painstaking way that beetles do when they are drunk on sugar-water. Others had simply keeled over among the flowers. The musicians drooped over their timbrels without enough oxygen between them for a trumpet-call or a groggy drum-tap. Then all of us, suddenly realizing, set up a shout and hurled ourselves towards the life-distributing oxygen pump.

With your permission I will draw a veil over the disgraceful scenes that ensued among the combatants. Dovebasket was knocked out. The Canadian Air Attaché had a collar-bone bruised. The egregious Serge escaped unscathed. A number of bottles were broken. Such language. Life has its ugly side, I suppose. But the main thing was that the Corps lived again, breathed again, could hold up its aching head once more. But one is hardly trained to live dangerously. Nevertheless, I noticed that not one dip failed to make a note of the wine of his choice. It would have been too much to miss that free crate. Some, in default of pencil and paper, had managed to scribble on their dickeys with lipstick. Polk-Mowbray, though beaten to his knees, nevertheless had the presence of mind to write Stella Polaris 1942 on his. Bloody, but relatively unbowed, you see.

And, as a matter of fact, after prayers the next day it was he who summed it all up rather neatly by saying: "And remember that in Peace, in War, in Love and in Diplomacy one thing is needful. I do not, I think, need to tell you what that is."

He didn't. It would have been labouring the point. We knew only too well. The Stiff Upper Lip.

A titanic battle now began

3

The Game's the Thing

As for Sport (said Antrobus), the very word makes me uneasy. I've never believed in its healing power. Once I was forced to referee a match between H.M.S. Thread-bare and the French Fleet which resulted in my nearly being dismembered. Luckily the Gents in the pavilion had a bolt and padlock on it or I wouldn't be here today. No. I regard Sport with Grave Reserve.

Polk-Mowbray was not of my opinion; he believed in the stuff. Thereby hangs my tale. It was during one of those long unaccountable huffs between ourselves and the Italians. You know the obscure vendettas which break out between Missions? Often they linger on long after the people who threw the first knife have been posted away. I have no idea how this huff arose. I simply inherited it from bygone dips whose bones were now dust. It was in full swing when I arrived—everyone applying freezing-mixture to the Italians and getting the Retort Direct in exchange. When you saw an Italian at a party you gave a slow smile amputated by scorn. Yes, we made

29

it clear that we were pretty miffed about something. They also acted in a markedly miffed manner. Yet I doubt if anyone on either side could have explained why we were all so dashed miffed. So while bows were still exchanged for protocol reasons they were only, so to speak, from above the waist. A mere contortion of the dickey, if you take me, as a tribute to manners. A slight Inclination accompanied by a *moue*. Savage work, old lad, savage work!

One day, however, the wind changed. Polk-Mowbray called a senior conference. "We must end this huff," he said regretfully. "Though it goes against the grain. London says that these dastards are going to vote against us at UNO. We must put aside our private pleasures and do everything to soothe and mollify the dogs. Our duty calls on us to surrender Our All." Several ideas for promoting the peace were put up, and at last—O fatal Dovebasket! —there came one which fired Polk-Mowbray's imagination." That's it!" he cried. "Brilliant! Magistral! Prescient! Dovebasket, I salute you! You will go far."

The idea was this: to challenge the Italian Mission to a football match and lose it gracefully, thus making them feel happy and well-disposed. Now everyone knew that the Italian Chancery was staffed by three guards who had been professionals once—footballers of international pointlessness. The team was a formidable one. To this we would oppose a scratch team of dead-beat dips who would be run off their feet in quarter of an hour, thus losing by two hundred goals to nothing. Like all Dovebasket's schemes it seemed sound on the face of it, almost ingenious. I had an obscure premonition of doom but I brushed it aside. What could go wrong with such an idea? I did not of course know (none of us did) that two of our

own Chancery Guards, Morgan and Bolster, were also
internationals and had played for Wales. Furthermore I
did not know that Dovebasket was short of money. True
he was always hanging about the Chancery sucking the
silver head of a swagger-stick and saying: "I'm fearfully
pushed for lolly these days." I paid no attention, being
somewhat pushed myself. Afterwards it all became clear.
Dovebasket and De Mandeville were in league. No
sooner was the match declared on than they began taking
bets *against* instead of *for* the Italians.

Innocently we pushed on with our preparations for
this senseless frolic unaware of the trap they were setting
for us. Polk-Mowbray spent quite a lot of money from
the Secret Service Vote to buy us blue shorts with a
polka-dot design and singlets of red-white-and-blue. I
don't suppose we made much of a showing as we bowled
on to the field to the polite hand-claps of the Ladies of the
Corps. Most of us had that dreadful rinsed-out look
which comes from Conferences. We had all constructed
heavy shin-pads from the Master-Files. I had nearly a
week's economic despatches down each stocking. Of
course with all this defensive equipment we moved like
pregnant water-buffaloes. Without grace, without poetry.
But we tried to look as if we meant business.

I must say the three Italian forwards filled me with the
liveliest anxiety. They were very large indeed and I
noticed that they had long-handled knives in their stock-
ings. I was rather glad that we were all set to lose. The
two Ambassadors elected to goal-keep because Heads of
Mission don't like to be seen hurrying. All were at last
assembled. The pitch was ankle deep in mud and within
a moment the ball resembled a half-mixed cake so that
even Arturo, Benjamino and Luigi had some difficulty in

pushing it about. It was even harder for us. After a few minutes of desultory running about we were all pretty winded and dispersed while the Italians executed some dashing figures of eight all round us, steadily moving down upon the anxious Polk-Mowbray—remorseless as an enema, old man.

Our defence was of the open-work variety and within a very few minutes they had scored a goal. Then another. Then another. Everyone beamed and resisted an impulse to cheer. We embraced them. They embraced us. Polk-Mowbray insisted on planting a fraternal kiss upon the Italian Ambassador's cheek. He, poor man, was deeply moved and clearly no longer miffed in the least. You can say what you like but we British know how to lose gamely. Prefer it, in fact. We had all taken on that frightfully decent look as we puffed about, showing ourselves plucky but inept—in fact in character. Our ladies cheered shrilly and waved their umbrellas.

By half-time we were seven goals down. Singularly few mishaps had occurred. True the Naval Attaché on the wing (who believed in reincarnation) was badly hacked by a free-thinking third secretary, but nobody gave a fig about that. We were losing, that was the main thing. It was not until half-time that Dovebasket's dastardly plan came into action. He and De Mandeville gracefully circulated the refreshments—rum cocktails and acid drops—before announcing their intention of retiring from the game "to give the replacements a chance". Both, it seemed, had slipped a disc. Polk-Mowbray was sympathetic, suspected nothing. "What bad luck," he cried. And as the whistle went I saw the military attaché's jeep approaching among the trees with the replacements in it. Two huge figures—Morgan and Bolster—sat in the back, armed *cap à pie* for the fray. "Well, well, Chancery Guards," cried Polk-Mowbray democratically. "What an awfully good show! That will freshen us up." Little did he know. . . .

They were huge, old man. I'd never seen them undressed before, so to speak. Such thews. Knotted and gnarled. Real Henry Moore jobs both. And covered in tattooing as well—ships and crowns and girl-friends' phone-numbers. Worst of all they both wore an air of surly magnificence that can only come from long leisurely potions of Navy Issue rum. They gave off waves of jaunty and illicit self-confidence. My heart began to sink as I watched these case-hardened male-nurses come trotting across the bog to take their place in our forward line. My blood froze as I heard Morgan whisper hoarsely: "Now remember we've got to do them proper or Dovie won't give us our cut, see?" So that was it! A cry broke from my lips. It was drowned by the whistle. We were off like men struggling for life in an ocean of glue.

What a titanic battle now began between the opposing forwards! The collisions in mid-air, the feints, the sorties, the trapeze-acts! Our innocent little game of push-ball suddenly took on a starker aspect; it was becoming more like a medieval butchery in a tilt-yard. The compatriots of Toscanini sent up musical cries of amazement at this sudden passionate flowering of a skill they did not guess we owned. By a brilliant system of double-entry Morgan and Bolster shot four goals in just over five minutes. Polk-Mowbray began to look faintly alarmed. The Italians, recovering from their surprise, buckled down to the job. The barges, the elbowing, the rabbit-punches on the referee's blind side began to increase. It was clear that we were losing our amateur status at last. Morgan and

Bolster were used to this. For them it was just like wind-ing in a capstan. Counter-barges and counter-shoves followed with the occasional dull thwack of a rabbit-punch. Cries of, "Foul" and, "You keek me, yes?" Two more goals to our credit. "By thunder!" cried Polk-Mowbray passionately. "What is going on?" Well might he ask. Bolster and Morgan were now playing with the concentrated fury of religious fanatics who had glimpsed the Promised Land. I don't know how much money was at stake. The Italians too had begun to get pretty rough. The pace had also increased. Clash followed upon clash. "Great Heavens!" cried Polk-Mowbray feebly. "Have they not been briefed, the Guards?" Yes, they had; but alas, not in the intended sense.

There was ten minutes to go when Bolster equalized. A groan went up from Italians and British alike. The Italian Ambassador burst into tears. Arturo began to finger the knife in his stocking and mutter. I felt quite faint just looking at him. The whistle again. By now everyone seemed to have become infected by pure rage. I received a kick from De Ponzo (ordinarily the mildest of men, a father, a bird-watcher)—a kick which left traces. I'll show you some time. In fact from a diplomatic football match the thing was steadily becoming a spec-tacle of unbridled bestiality. Such pushing, such cuffing, such heaving and bumping I have never witnessed before or since. And the language—a Saturnalia of Swearing, old man. If I hadn't been so scared I would have blushed to the roots of my C.M.G. Then at last it came—the dire *coup de grâce*.

Bolster opened fire with a boom like a sixteen-inch gun right from the popping-crease as it were. There was cold and dire malevolence about the shot. The sodden leather fairly winged through the sky towards the uncorseted form of the Italian Chief Of Mission. Mind you, for an ethereal sort of man he was quite spirited and did not flinch. There was a hollow concussion followed by a yell as our distinguished colleague received the charge full in the midriff. I felt things going black all round me. What a shot! Yes, and what a casualty—for the poor Ambassador, propelled backwards through his own goal by the sheer force of this flying pudding, was soon lying senseless in the ditch. It seemed to me that all they could do now was to draw a mackintosh reverently over the body before resuming play—as they do at Twickenham. *We were now leading by one goal.* Imagine our despair! Polk-Mowbray was dancing with rage and consternation in our goalmouth. The ladies were screaming shrilly. Drage was holding a mirror to the Italian Ambassador's lips and shaking his head sadly. On all sides rose cries for help. Messengers began running in all directions for ambulances.

And it was now that the tactless Bolster cried merrily: "Another eight minutes to go." And this tore it, to use a vulgar phrase, tore it good and proper right down the centre. The Italian forwards closed in on him with the manifest intention of wiping the smile from his lips. Morgan intervened. Blows began to be exchanged. The Naval Attaché was struck down. Other peacemakers tried unwisely to intervene. The referee was gouged and swallowed the pea in his whistle. A scuffle now started destined to end in a riot. Knives were drawn. There were slashes and screams. The ladies shrieked in unison. It was nearly ten minutes before the Vulgarian Flying-Squad arrived and surged on to the pitch armed with tommy-guns. We were all under arrest. We were ignominiously handcuffed together for nearly an hour before the *doyen* could persuade them that we were privileged dips and not subject to the civil penalties of riot. Those not on the list—our forwards and theirs—were carried away in a plain van. The whole thing ended in a scandal.

And our neat little plan? What is there to add? The vote went against us at UNO, and the Italians stayed miffed. To add insult to injury Dovebasket's Christmas Card that year showed a Father Xmas in football-boots. Yes, of course they stayed miffed. I bet you the miff remains unrequited to this day.

No, you'll never catch me joking about sport.

A two-to-one Martini

4

Something à la Carte?

The tragedy of Mungo Piers-Foley is one (said Antrobus) which should give every Thoughtful Person Pause. It did me. It still does. By the purest inadvertency he found himself cast into the Bottomless Pit. He was a bit absent-minded that day. Yet what happened to him could happen to any of us.

Mungo was posted to us from the Blues as Military Attaché, and he was a gallant and carefree young colonel, full of the spice of life. You felt that he had a rich inner nature if only he could be persuaded to open his mouth. He was one of those mournful cylindrical men with hair parted in the middle—men who say little but think a lot. Yet who knows what they think? I don't. But he was an officer and a gentleman of unblemished reputation and a sportsman to boot. Not only to boot, to saddle as well. He had what is known as a splendid seat. He rode to hounds. However pointless the point-to-point, Mungo would be there, clearing hurdle after hurdle on his thoroughbred mule. He played polo without ever once

39

hitting his horse. Myself I don't know much about horses, and what little I know seems to me singularly charmless. The last time I went hacking with Polk-Mowbray I got left in a tree for roughly the same reasons as Absalom. But that is neither here nor there. . . .

Mungo had won a huge collection of cups and saucers which he wore on his mantelpiece. He shot. He dynamited fish. An all-round sportsman if ever there was one. We were proud of him in the Mission. All this, of course, only made his tragedy harder cheese than ever. It happened while he was in Paris for a week to help reorganize the NATO cavalry to face the threat of a rocket age. On the morning of his return he lurched into my office looking like a lot of overlooked washing-up. "Antrobus," he said, "Hear my story. I am finished, old thing, absolutely finished. I've just put in my resignation and left Polk-Mowbray in tears." He sat down and fumbled for one of my cigars.

"It happened while I was in Paris," he said. "Quite inadvertent, the whole dashed thing. It could have happened to anyone. I popped into the Octagon for a bite. It wasn't until the *addition* came that I realized. Old man, *I had eaten a piece of horse!*"

I sprang up, startled. "You *what*?" I cried incredulously, realizing that I was in the presence of tragedy.

"Horse," he repeated wearily, passing his hand over his forehead. "As I live, Antrobus, a slice carved from a geegee. It all seems like a horrible dream. Yet I must say it cut quite sweetly and the sauce was so dashed good that I didn't realize it. It was only when the bill came that the whole of my past life flashed before my eyes. Dear God— a horse! And I a Colonel in the Blues! I was so surprised you could have poured me out with a spoon."

I groaned in sympathy. He gave a harsh cracked laugh and went on. "To think of it, I who have lived for, and practically on, horses. The irony of it all. To find myself sitting there, involuntarily wrapped round a succulent slice of fetlock, feeling the world's biggest bounder. And with a touch of mustard, too." He shuddered at the memory.

"But surely," I said, looking as always for the Silver Lining, "you are hardly to be blamed, Mungo. Surely you could have absorbed just one slice and then Hushed Everything Up? No-one could find it in his heart to blame you."

He shook his head sadly. "I thought of that," he said, "but my conscience wouldn't give me any rest, Antrobus. After all, here I am, a founder-member of the Society For The Prevention Of Everything To Nags. Old Boy, I was largely instrumental in getting all those country houses set aside for aged horses, for getting them into the Health Service, for getting them painted by Munnings before they Passed On. Why, we were hoping to get one into Parliament this year. . . . How could I strike my colours, go back on my basic principles? I admit I thought of it. After all, I have eaten many strange things in un-guarded moments. I once ate some smoked grandmother in the Outer Celebes, but that was to save the regimental goat. And once at Government House in Gibraltar I *think* I ate a portion of infant monkey. But it was never proved. The A.D.C. refused to confess. But all this is a far cry from horses, old chap. A different world. No, I confess that I sobbed aloud as I paid that bill."

For a moment he was silent, and then went on. "After that, Antrobus, there came an endless chain of sleepless nights. I brooded, old man. No peace. At times I thought I might go and throw myself on the mercy of Elizabeth

David, confessing everything to her frankly, hiding no-thing, asking for absolution. But when I mugged up her books I found no references to anything more question-able than eels or bloater paste—revolting enough, but mundane compared to what I was up against. No, there was no way out. I realized that I should have to Face the Music. So I did. I confess it hurt. I resigned from Whites and Boodles. I had myself crossed off every Stud Book in the Shires. The Athenaeum will see me no more. I even closed my account with the Army, Navy and Air-Force Stores. I transferred my overdraft. I confessed all to the Pytchley and did a public penance at Hurlingham. Then I broke my saddle over my knee . . . and all was over. I am a broken man, Antrobus. I simply came back to collect my gongs and brasses. I only popped in to say good-bye. I somehow felt you would understand."

I was deeply moved. But what could I say to comfort and console poor Mungo? Little enough in all conscience. He still had a fortnight to carry his bat until a replacement arrived and all this time he spent in strict purdah, refusing all invitations. There was only one little incident which, in the light of subsequent events, seems to me significant. It proved how deeply he had been marked by this Major Experience. His inhibitions had begun to slough off. De Mandeville reported that Mungo had been seen in a local hotel dining on *octopus*. I could hardly believe it. *Octopus!* The stuff that comes like ectoplasm! But this was the only straw in the wind. After that, silence closed in. Then Mungo left us and passed out of memory. As the years went by I often thought of him with a twinge of compas-sion. Doubtless he was in some far-enough-flung colony to dine openly on yams and white mice. I saluted his gallantry in my heart.

SOMETHING À LA CARTE?

But now here is the grisly sequel to my tale. Spalding used to go to Kenya every year to see his family and shoot a bit. One year he went up-country on *safari*. In the heart of the jungle, in a clearing, before a modest hut of wattle, he came upon a dinner-jacketed figure having a pre-prandial. "Mungo!" he cried. Yes, it was Mungo. He had hidden his shame in that remote corner. They embraced warmly and Spalding was glad to see that his character still had a few fibres intact—for he was correctly dressed for dinner. They sat down on camp-stools and discussed a two-to-one Martini which Mungo mixed with all his old *flair*. Though he had aged he still looked fairly steady on his pins, and he still made the sort of Martini which fairly whistles through the rigging. Heartening signs, these.

It was only when the brain-fever birds began to call and the little radio in the corner struck eight o'clock that Spalding Suddenly Understood that it wasn't, it couldn't be, the old Mungo. . . . For his host said, quite distinctly: "Why not stay and have pot-luck with me tonight? We have elephant for dins." *Elephant!*

Spalding paled—he had been very strictly brought up. Was it possible that Mungo was sitting out here in the wilds gorging himself on elephant? (And if so, how was it done? It must take ages to marinate?) He gulped loudly. "Did I understand you to say elephant, Mungo?" he said.

"Yes," said Mungo, with a kind of loose grin. "You see, old boy, there is no such thing as a *cuisine* in Africa. Once one leaves the Old Country one achieves a kind of Universality, a Oneness with Nature. HERE EVERY-THING IS EDIBLE." He spread his arms to the night, knocking over his glass. "If you don't like elephant," he went on, "I can organize squirrel or chipmunk or boa-constrictor. It's all one. I just send out a little man with a blow-pipe and it's all yours."

Spalding shuddered and muttered a prayer under his breath. "Yes," went on Mungo, "I gave away my Bou-lestin and both my Elizabeth David's. They are no use here except for missionaries who have Outworn Con-cepts. Personally I use Buffon's Natural History to give me ideas for my meals. Why, just to leaf through Section One (Primates) stimulates the appropriate juice, gives one an appetite. I say, you've turned awfully pale. You aren't ill, are you?"

"No, no," said Spalding, "it is simply the kerosene light shining on my rather high and pale forehead."

Mungo settled himself on his camp-stool and said: "Yes, old boy. If once the readers of *The Times* found out just how Edible everything is, it would be all up with the Wine and Food Society." Then in a slow, dreamy voice, full of naked *luxe* and *volupté*, he began to recite softly: "Leeches *à la rémoulade*. . . . Giraffe *Truffée aux Oignons*. . . . Boa-constrictor *Chasseur*. . . . *Ragoût de Flamingo* with *Water-Rat Flambé*. . . ." He was sunk in a deep trance.

Spalding could bear it no longer. He tip-toed out of the clearing and ran like a madman in the direction of Nairobi. . . .

Now I didn't tell you this story (said Antrobus) simply to upset you. No. Moreover, I hope you won't repeat it. I should hate it to get back to the Household Cavalry. It simply illustrates the sort of thing one is up against in the Service. The next Christmas, when my Aunt Hetty asked me to choose two quotations for a sampler she was making me, it was really with Mungo in mind that I made my choice. One text reads: "By their Menus shall ye know them." And the other: "Nothing Exceeds like Excess"....

I trust you take my point?

The F.O.'s senior courier running howling across the town

5

Where the Bee Sucks...

One is at a loss (said Antrobus) when one looks back on those rough old times to account for the thin but rich vein of fatuity which ran through the character of Polk-Mowbray. Though in many ways an admirable Chief of Mission, a talented and self-disciplined man, nevertheless, he was in others simply a babe in arms, old boy, a babe in arms.

The main thing I think was that he was subject to Sudden Urges. He was over-imaginative, he was highly-strung. One week for example it would be Sailors' Knots. It was all right so long as he only sat at his desk playing with string but this was not all. He grew reckless, ambitious, carried away by all this new knowledge. He took to demonstrating his powers at children's parties, charity bazaars, cocktails—everywhere. And the awful thing was that his tricks never worked. He trussed the German Ambassador's eldest son up so tightly that the child nearly suffocated; we just released him in time with the help of the garden shears. Drage had to pour a pail of

sweet iced Cup all over the little swollen Teuton face to
revive the brat. Then Polk-Mowbray tied himself to the
Embassy door-knob and could not disengage. Quite a
crowd gathered. It was humiliating. Once more we had
to resort to the shears. I took to keeping a pair of them
handy in my office. As Head of Chancery you can imagine
how my responsibilities weighed upon me. . . .

"Antrobus," he used to say to me as he sat abstractedly
making love-knots in a length of high quality manila.
"Antrobus I am in the wrong profession. Only just
realized it. I should have been sent to sea as a youth.
Round the Cape in a sou'wester, what? That should have
been my life, Antrobus." Who was I, as his junior, to
contradict?

Two days later I came in to find his typist spliced to the
Chancery radiator by one swollen wrist. She was in tears.
Polk-Mowbray could not release her and nor could I.
"Tut tut," he kept saying. "And such a simple little running bowline too. It is most vexing. I was just trying to
show Angela a wrinkle or two." In the end, Morgan the
Chancery guard was forced to pull the radiator out of the
wall to free her. Water poured out into De Mandeville's
office and ruined a Persian carpet he prized. Obviously
things had gone far enough. We had a secret meeting and
delegated to Butch Benbow, the Naval Attaché, the task
of crushing this little hobby before the whole Corps was
infected by it. We knew that in his present mood Polk-
Mowbray reverenced all seafaring men—even if they
were martyrs to sea-sickness as Butch Benbow was. . . . I
must say, though, he was clever, was Butch. But then you
can always count on the Navy. He asked Polk-Mowbray
outright whether he wasn't *afraid* to go on playing with
string at such a rate—and on such a scale?

"Afraid?" said the Chief Of Mission mildly. "Why afraid?"

"The last Ambassador to suffer from stringomania", said Butch earnestly, "hung himself." He went *krik krik* with his mouth and drew a string round his neck with his finger. Then, to complete the pantomime he rolled his eyes up into his skull until only the whites showed and stuck out a large—and I must say somewhat discoloured and contused tongue. "He's quite right, sir," I said. Polk-Mowbray looked from one to the other, quite startled. "But sailors do it all the time," he said.

"Sailors can untie themselves when they wish," said Butch somewhat stiffly. "Besides they don't walk in their sleep like you do, sir. The Ambassador I spoke of was also a sleep-walker." This really made Polk-Mowbray jump. It was one of those lucky hits. Actually he had only once walked in his sleep—though the result was disastrous. I'll tell you about it sometime. It was after a prawn curry devised by De Mandeville. He sat staring at us for a long time with popping eye. Then he sighed regretfully and we knew that for him the days of sail were numbered.

"Thank you for your solicitude," he said.

Well, that was only an example: I really wanted to tell you about the infernal bees. One day I walked into his office and found him clad for the most part in a bee-keeper's veil and gauntlets and holding a sort of tuning-fork with which, as I understand it, you pick up the Queen. I was aghast, but he only waved airily and told me to sit down. "Antrobus," he said, "I have the answer to the monotony of this post. The murmur of innumerable bees, dear boy. A *pastoral* hobby, suitable for diplomats. Something that harms no-one, and which yields honey for tea." All around him lay magazines and brochures entitled *Profitable Bee Keeping, The Hornet and Bee Guide, The Bee-Fancier*—and that sort of thing. It was clear that he had been delving deeply into bee lore. "I have ordered a hive from Guernsey," he said, "and asked the Bag Room to send them on." "The Bag Room," I faltered. "But surely livestock is on the proscribed list?" The people who make up the Diplomatic Bag as you know are pretty touchy and there are endless rules and regulations about what you can and can't send by bag. Polk-Mowbray shook his head. "I've looked up the regulations," he said, "there is nothing about bees. The chief prohibition is on liquids, but a hive of bees isn't liquid." I doubted the soundness of his reasoning. Liquids were proscribed because once in the old days a young attaché had sent a bottle of inferior Chianti back to his mother and it had exploded. Most of Lord Cromer's despatches had to be hung out to dry before serving, and some of them actually turned green. The bottle must have been sinfully corked. But then Italian wine. . . . Anyway, I still didn't like to think of the Bag Room trustingly accepting a cardboard box with a few holes in the top. "What if they make honey among the confidential despatches?" I said. He laughed airily. "Pouf!" he said. "There will be no difficulty about that. You will see."

I said no more. Seven days later a disgraceful scene took place on the platform at Venice. The bees, maddened by their solitude in the bag, broke out and stormed into the first-class carriage where Fothergill the courier was eating a ham sandwich. They stung him. He, poor fellow, was attached by a padlock to the sack and could not free himself in time. The next thing was the spectacle of the F.O.'s senior courier running howling across the town waving a bag out of which poured bees and confidential reports in ever increasing quantities. The other couriers, in a vain attempt to help followed him in a sort of demonic paper-chase which only ended at St. Marks, where Fothergill took sanctuary behind the altar. Here the darkness foxed the bees and they turned their attention to the priests. And our mail? Old man, it was all at the bottom of the Grand Canal. The consul general was forced to set out with a fleet of gondolas to rescue it before it fell into Unauthorized Hands. You can imagine what a scandal. Fothergill arrived beeless and bagless and under a threat of Excommunication. I thought this would cure Polk-Mowbray. Not a bit. The next lot were sent out by air in an airtight container and Drage was sent to meet them at the airport. A hive had been rigged up in the garage and Polk-Mowbray walked about the Residence in his veil waiting for his blasted bees with feverish professional impatience. At last the moment came. He knew just how to tip them out, and so on. But the bees took violent exception to the hive and within a matter of seconds were darkening the sky. They flew round and round in a desultory fashion at first and then with a roar flew into a drainpipe and emerged in the Chancery where they settled in the old tin stove by the bookcase. For a while everyone was on guard but the little creatures were quite well behaved. "Live and let live," cried Polk-Mowbray sucking his thumb. (He had been stung.) "If the brutes want to live here we shall respect their wishes." "I thought it a bit hard on the junior secretaries but what could I say?

But somewhat to my surprise the bees gave no trouble whatsoever; indeed as time went on their subdued murmuring helped rather than hindered the composition of despatches. Polk-Mowbray rather lost interest in them: from time to time he would put on his veil and peer up the stove-pipe, calling upon them to be good boys and come out for a fly round, but much to everyone's relief they ignored him. Gradually nobody thought of them at all. But alas! This was not to be the end of the story. When the bees finally did emerge they created unparalleled havoc. It was all due to a new secretary, Sidney Trampelvis, who had been insufficiently briefed, and who, on a whim, filled the stove with old betting slips he no longer needed and blithely set them alight. Now at this time there was one of those Ineffably Delicate Conferences taking place in the committee-room, presided over by no less a personage than Lord Valerian—you know, the Treasury chap. It was all about a trade pact—I must not reveal the details. Now this fellow Valerian—rather a bounder I thought—for some reason awed Polk-Mowbray. I don't know why. Perhaps he had highly placed relations in the F.O. Perhaps it was his enormous beard which hung down like a fire curtain and only parted occasionally when he moved to reveal a strip of O.E. tie. Typical of course. The rumour was that he used to wear his O.E. tie in bed, over his pyjama jacket. Well, we Wykehamists can only raise a lofty eyebrow over this sort of gossip—which by the way we never repeat. Well, there we all were in solemn conclave when there arose a confused shouting from the Chancery where Trampelvis was receiving the first thrust, so to speak. There followed a moment of silence during which Valerian cleared his throat and was about to launch himself again, and then there came a tremendous hum followed by the sound of running feet. I did not know Drage was capable of such a turn of speed. Into the room he bounded—perhaps with

some vague idea of saving his Chief, perhaps of issuing a
general gale warning. But it was too late. They were upon
us in a compact and lethal cloud, flying very low and with
stings at the ready. The confusion was indescribable.
Have you ever seen *bees* on a fighter sweep, old boy?
Ever felt them crawling up your trousers, down your
collar, into your waistcoat? One would have to have
nerves of steel not to shriek aloud. To judge by the noises
we started making it would be clear that diplomatic
nerves are made not so much of steel as of raffia. People
began beating themselves like old carpets. Polk-Mowbray
after one plaintive cry of, "My bees," seized a poker and
started behaving like Don Quixote with a set of particularly irritating windmills. Drage lapsed into Welsh religious verse punctuated by snarls and a sort of involuntary
pole-jumping. I hid myself in the curtains and extinguished
the bees as hard as I could. But the awful thing was that
the Queen (I imagine it was her) made a bee-line (to coin
a metaphor) for the Drury Lane beard of Lord Valerian
who as yet had not fully grasped the situation. He looked
down with ever-growing horror to find them swarming
blithely in it, with the obvious intention of setting up
house there. He was too paralysed to move. (I think personally that he used to spray his beard with Eau de
Portugal before committee meetings and this must have
attracted the Queen.) Mind you this all happened in a
flash. Polk-Mowbray, what with guilt and solicitude for
Valerian, was almost beside himself; no sacrifice, he felt,
was too great to save the day. In a flash of gallantry he
seized the garden shears which had been lying on the
mantelpiece (pitiful relic of the days when he played
with string) and with a manful though ragged snip . . .
divested the Chairman of both beard and O.E. tie at one

and the same stroke . . . I cannot say it improved Valerian's
temper any more than his appearance—Polk-Mowbray
had sliced rather badly. But there it was. Walking
wounded had to retire to the buttery for a Witch Hazel
compress. The bees, having done their worst, flew out of
the window and into the Ministry of Foreign Affairs
across the road. I did not wait to see the sequel. I was so
grateful for emerging from this business unscathed that I
tip-toed back to my office and rang down to the buttery.
I don't mind admitting that I ordered a Scotch and Soda,
and a stiffer one than usual. I would even admit (under
pressure, and *sotto voce*) that you might have seen a faint,
fugitive smile graven upon my lips. I was not entirely
displeased, old man, with Polk-Mowbray's method of
dealing with an O.E. tie. In my view it was the only one.
Was it, I wondered, too much to hope that it might become More General?

Polk-Mowbray got a terrific electric shock

The Unspeakable Attaché

It was (said Antrobus) a bit before your time—mercifully for you. The creature was posted just before you arrived. Now of this fellow, Trevor Dovebasket (he was then assistant Military Attaché), I have only this to say: it was clear that the youth was in league with the Devil. Some fearful Faustian compact had taken place. You could tell from his appearance—eyebrows meeting in the middle. It was clear from the way that he bit his nails that he read *Popular Mechanics* in secret. More, his office was always full of meccano and string. He was always tampering with electrical circuits, fuses, and using that beastly sticky stuff and so on. A really vicious streak. One day Polk-Mowbray got a terrific electric shock off his telephone. Then some Juliets exploded under the noses of the Rotary Club causing grave loss of morale. It was never proved, of course, but I knew. . . . Something told me it was Dovebasket.

He was in league with the Devil on one side and De Mandeville on the other. Together they organized a form

57

of beetle-racing in the Chancery. Beetles with electro-magnets tied to their tails, if you please. Imagine my concern. The beetles were named after us. They made a book and encouraged betting wholesale. Dolly Pusey, the new cipherine, gambled away a year's unearned increments and most of the fruits of the F.O. Pension Scheme in a matter of minutes. When I found out I had no option but to return her to London. But that was not all. . . .

They invented an electric train for serving food and sold the idea to Drage as a labour-saving device. The train ran on to the dining-table and stopped before the diners with a plate on each carriage. On the face of it it seemed ingenious. It was worked by buttons from Polk-Mowbray's place. Mind you, I had my doubts. But as there was an Electrical Trades Union Conference and we had some of its members to lunch Polk-Mowbray (who had a childish streak) thought he would impress them with his little toy. You have guessed? It was not until the *Bombe Surprise* was loaded that the machinery went wrong. There was a frightful accident, the train was de-railed into our laps, and the *Bombe* (a marvellous creation on which Drage had spent all night) lived up to its name . . . De Mandeville got Number One Field Punishment. He had to feed the goldfish in the Residence for a month.

Well, this is only to show you what I was up against with this fellow Dovebasket. At this time the Corps was going through one of its Little Phases. Dips are a some-what emulous tribe as you know, always trying to vie with one another. That winter it was dogs. The Hun-garians led off. Their Labour Attaché suddenly appeared with some colossal greyhounds from the Steppes. He allowed himself to be towed about in public by them wearing a somewhat fanciful air. At once everyone got emulous. In a matter of weeks the dog market was booming. Everyone had dogs of various sizes and shapes: huge ones, little ones, squashed-looking ones and ones that looked like cold rissoles. The French went in for topiary jobs, the Italians for the concertina shape, the British for those great torpid brutes which carry Hennessy's Brandy round in artful little barrels. I forget their names. They rescue people from snowdrifts by licking their faces and dealing out a much-needed tot at the right time. Horrible. The Albanians produced some green-fanged sheepdogs so fierce that they had to be kept tied to trees in the grounds and fed by a system of underarm bowling until a shepherd was found who understood their natures. He took them for walks on a length of steel hawser.

Well, this was all very well, had not Polk-Mowbray been fired by the idea of a Diplomatic Dog-Show. He was always easily led and this fellow Dovebasket fired him with thoughts of winning a first prize in the barrel-pushing class. I viewed the whole thing with concern, but I could not guess from which quarter the blow might fall. Anyway, they worked out a splendid dog-show at which every Mission would win the first prize of its class and all our honours be simultaneously saved. Rosettes, buttons, marking-cards—everything was thought out. A firm of dog-biscuit manufacturers was persuaded to put up some rather depressing prizes in the form of dog-statuettes in pressed steel which De Mandeville painted with gold leaf to make look more expensive. The Town Hall was engaged for the *venue* and the press was fed with a great deal of advance information in the form of news-flashes which it did not use. Speeches were carefully worked up containing the requisite number of Tactful Phrases about Everything. The ladies of the Corps decided to make it a contest of dresses as well as dogs. Many were the clever little creations run up overnight, many the models flown from Paris. The air was full of excitement. It was the first Spring engagement. Sewing machines hummed night and day. The Minister For Interior was invited to give away the prizes—there was one for each Chief Of Mission. Polk-Mowbray went through agonies of excitement practising his Few Words Of Thanks in the Residence pier-glass. Altogether it looked like a pleasurable and harmonious afternoon. But . . . there was a look in Dovebasket's eye I misliked. Could it be, I wondered, that the fellow was Up To Something? One never knew. I confess that there was a still small voice within me which whispered "Something is bound to give" as I studied the (I must say) very creditable lay-out of the Town Hall, gay with the flags of every nation and made brilliant by the courtly presence of Our Ladies in their prettiest frocks. The day was fine and sunny. The dogs were extremely even tempered, wagging their grotesque stumps and coloured ribbons as the solemn group of judges circulated marking down points on their embossed cards. Cocktails were coming up thick and fast.

It was at this point that I distinctly heard De Mandeville say in the hoarse undertone. "Let her go now, Dovie." Together the two retreated to a high stand above the *mêlée* while a look of intense interest came over their faces. Dovebasket appeared to have a cold and put a handkerchief to his face. He appeared to blow his nose. Suddenly a quiver of anguish appeared to run through the canine population like a wind in corn. The Albanian sheep-dogs gave one long quivering howl like an Alban Berg violin solo and then . . . all hell broke loose. These peaceable amiable dogs suddenly turned upon their masters and the judges, seething with an inexplicable rage. They turned upon one another. Cries and tumult arose. Stands were overturned. The sheep dogs went into action against the Labradors, the Airedales against the Fox terriers. Owners were dragged hither and thither by their leashes which got inextricably mixed up with chairs and legs and dips. Bites of all sizes and depths were registered. Blood began to flow, tempers to rise. The Russians began to shake their fists. The Minister was bitten in his . . . seat of office. Polk-Mowbray lost a spat to a shaggy mixed-up Borzoi. Lap-dogs squealed like piccolos, the bigger brutes bayed, the diplomats moaned, positively moaned.

In a single bound I was at Dovebasket's side. I whipped the handkerchief from his face. "Unmasked," I hissed. It was just as I thought. He was blowing hard upon one of those whistles which, while inaudible to the human ear, produced a high-pitched buzz calculated to unnerve dogs. "It was simply an experiment," he said with a sickly smile, "De Mandeville betted me an even tenner that my whistle wouldn't work."

"Experiment!" I cried. "Look around you, you wretched youth." The scene was a terrible one to witness. I have not seen anything to equal it—except perhaps once when someone released a grass-snake at a Pen Club Conference in Venice. I turned upon Dovebasket. "Give me that foul instrument," I cried in a voice of thunder. "I confiscate it. And as soon as it is safe to get down I shall conduct you to your Chief of Mission."

But he only smirked. He was incorrigible, the little blackhead. When later that day I told Polk-Mowbray about the whistle he was beside himself with rage. "Dove-

basket must go," he said in ringing tones. And duly—
these things take an age to arrange—Dovebasket went.
He was promoted to the rank of Senior Military Attaché
in Delhi. Upwards, old boy. It's always upwards in the
service. That is perhaps the tragedy of it all.

The Thumb . . . was an iron one

The Iron Hand

Have you ever noticed (said Antrobus) that people called Percy are almost invariably imbeciles? Perhaps the name confers a fateful instability upon the poor souls; perhaps it is chosen as the most appropriate for those who, from birth, show all the signs of being lathe-turned morons.... Anyway it is a fact. Hearing the name I know I need never look at the face. I am sure of the ears spread to the four winds like banana-leaves, sure of the lustreless eyes, the drooling mouth, hammer-toes and so on ... Percy is as Percy looks in my experience.

Nor was Percy, the Embassy second-footman, any exception. In fact to call him a footman was an insult to what is, after all, a *métier*. He was a superannuated potboy with the sort of face one sees slinking out of cinemas in places like Sidcup and Penge—idle, oafish and conceited. He spent hours tending the spitcurl on his receding forehead and complacently ogling the housemaids. He rode a bicycle round and round the flower-beds until Polk-Mowbray (bird-watching from his office) became giddy and ordered him to desist. He whistled with a dreadful monotonous shrillness. He chewed gum with a sickening rotary action that turned the beholder's stomach.

Well, when Drage went on leave the domestic arrangements of the Embassy were confided to this junior Quasimodo, and that is how the business of the iron hand came about. Normally Percy was never allowed to touch either the Embassy plate or the suit of armour which stood in the Conference Room and which we used to call "The White Knight". Personally I hated the thing, though Drage loved it dearly. It was always giving us frights during Secret Conferences. Once the beaver came down with a clang just as Polk-Mowbray was about to Come To A Decision and we all got a dreadful start. On another occasion smoke was seen curling out of its mouth and the cry of "Spy" went up from one and all. Trampelvis had dropped a cigar-end into it. After this I had it moved into the hall. Once a month Drage used to take it apart and polish it up. Now Percy had his glaucous eye fixed firmly upon "The White Knight", and no sooner had Drage left than he at once began to fool around with the thing.

He put the headpiece on and scared the housemaids by gargling at them through the buttery hatch after dark. He even went for a twilight ride on his bicycle dressed in the thing—out of one gate and in at the other—which made the startled Vulgarian sentries rub their eyes. Why they didn't shoot him I don't know. It must have seemed clear evidence that the Secret Service was going over on to the offensive—and one little arpeggio on a sub-machine gun would have saved us so much subsequent trouble. . . .

THE IRON HAND

Well, these benighted pranks went on until one day Percy met his Waterloo. After a successful appearance as Hamlet's father he regained the buttery one day, panting happily, and started to divest himself of helm and cod-piece in time to serve a pre-dinner Martini in the sitting-room. Judge the poor mawk's surprise when he found that the right hand wouldn't unscrew according to plan. All the wrenching and pulling in the world could not budge it. In a flash he realized that unless he cut along the dotted line this grotesque mailed fist was with him for life. The press-stud or what-have-you was jammed against the demi-quiver of the bassinet, more or less. The first I heard of it was a noise which suggested that someone was trying to shoe a mettlesome carthorse in the Residence—rustic, yet somehow out of keeping with Polk-Mowbray's ways. It didn't seem natural. It didn't fit into Our World. Listening more carefully I thought I heard the sound of human groans, and I was not wrong. The cry for a certified obstetrician had already been raised.

Percy was sobbing like a donkey, surrounded by frightened housemaids. He realized that he was dished. There he sat on the three-legged stool in the buttery, bathed in tears, and holding up this expensive-looking piece of ironmongery in dumb appeal. "Wretched oaf!" I cried. "You have been told a hundred times not to touch 'The White Knight'." I pulled and tugged, but it was no go; the iron boxing-glove was stuck clean as a cavalry boot. Various fruitless suggestions were made, various attempts to divest him were carried out. In vain. I took him into the Chancery in search of qualified advice. Spalding tried, De Mandeville tried. We pushed and pulled and heaved in unison. Percy sobbed more loudly. But the thing refused to yield. Polk-Mowbray and a couple of archivists made their appearance, intrigued by the noises from a normally sedate Chancery. They brought fresh blood and fresh impetus to his rescuers. While Polk-Mowbray stood on his chest we formed a human chain—like getting the Lowestoft Lifeboat in— and tried to wrest the article from him by brute force. It was no go. A little more and we should have shredded Frederick. A private socket would have given. "There's no need to yell so," said Spalding angrily. "We are only trying to help you." We desisted panting and had another conference. Dovebasket summoned the Embassy chauffeurs and took counsel with them. Now plans were formulated involving expensive and bizarre equipment— for they planned to saw their way in with a hacksaw and so deliver the lad. But they punctured him. Then Polk-Mowbray boldly tried to hammer the thing off with a croquet mallet. The noise was deafening, the result nil. I must say those medieval farriers, artificers—or whatever they were called—knew their business. It didn't look much, this olde worlde gauntlet, but heavens how it stuck. Percy was by now very much frightened and perhaps slightly bruised around the edges. We plied him with bonded gin to bring the roses back. There he sat in Spalding's swivel-chair, letting out a moan from time to time, and drinking thirstily. Occasionally one of us would have a new idea and advance upon him, whereupon he would swivel wildly in order to avoid further pain. In this way he dealt Butch Benbow a backhand stroke with his glove across the shoulders which felled our redoubtable Naval Attaché and kept him down for the count. More gin, more moans. There seemed to be no way out of the *impasse*. Time was running out. Guests were expected. "I've a good mind to dress you up in the rest of

this thing and send you back to your mother by air!"
cried Polk-Mowbray in a transport of fury. I felt for him.

The awful thing was that the Dutch were due to dine
with us that evening. It always seemed to be the fate of
the Dutch to be invited on crisis evenings. That evening
was a real *kermesse héroique*. Percy was a poor butler at the
best of times but tonight he bordered on the really
original. He shambled round and round the room sniffing,
half anaesthetized by gin and . . . well, you can imagine
our guests' faces when a mailed hand appeared over their
shoulder holding a soup-plate. They *must* have felt that
there was something uncanny about it. Clearly they
longed to pop a question but the Iron Laws of the Corps
forbade it. They held their curiosity in leash. They were
superb. Normally Percy always got his thumb in the soup
—but the thumb this evening was an iron one. I shudder
to recall it. Yet by a superhuman effort we remained
calm and Talked Policy as coolly as we could. The old
training dies hard. Somehow we managed to carry it off.
Yet I think our hosts felt themselves to be in the presence
of irremediable tragedy. They pressed our hands in silent
sympathy as we tucked them into their cars. All of a
sudden one felt terribly alone again—alone with the Iron
Hand. . . .

Well, my dear fellow, everyone had a go at that blasted
hand—the Chaplain, the cipher staff, finally the doctor.
The latter wanted to heat the whole thing up with a blow-
torch until the press-stud expanded but that would have
incinerated Percy. By this time, of course, I hardly cared
what they did to him. I would willingly have amputated
the arm from somewhere just above the waist, myself.
But meanwhile an urgent appeal had gone out to the
Museum for a professor of armour to advise us; but the

only available specialist in chain-mail was away in Italy on leave. He would not return for another two days. Two days! I know that it doesn't sound a great deal. But in the middle of the night Percy found that he had lost all trace of feeling in the arm. It had got pins and needles. He sat up in bed, haunted by a new terror. It seemed to him that gangrene had perhaps set in; he had heard the doctor muttering something about the circulation of the blood. . . . He bounded down the stairs into the Residence roaring like a lion and galloped into Polk-Mowbray's bedroom waving the object. Our esteemed Chief Of Mission, after the nervous strain of that evening, had turned in early, and was enjoying a spell of blameless slumber. Awakened by this apparition, and being unable to understand a word of Percy's gibberish, he jumped to the purely intuitive conclusion that a fire had broken out upstairs. It was a matter of moments to break glass and press button. Woken by that fateful ringing the Embassy are squads swept gallantly into life, headed by Morgan find Chowder, pyjama-clad and in steel helmets. Just how Percy and his Ambassador escaped a thorough foam-bath that night is a mystery to me. Neither seemed very coherent to the gallant little band of rescuers as they swept through the dining-room with their sprinklers and up the stairs.

At last order was restored and the doctor summoned, who did much to soothe Percy's fears. But he did on the other hand take a serious view of the pins and needles. The circulation was being impeded by the gauntlet apparently. Percy must somehow keep the blood flowing in it—keep the circulation going—until help from the outer world arrived. How? By banging it, if you please, banging it repeatedly on anything that was to hand, banging it day and night lest the gangrene set in. I tell you, my dear chap, that that fateful banging, which lasted two whole days and nights, rings in my ears even now. Banging on the walls, the buttery table, on the floor. Neither work nor sleep was possible. An army of poltergeists could not have done half as well. Bang, bang, bang . . . now loud and slow, now hollow and resonant, now sharp and clear. Day and night the banging haunted us until at last the Professor appeared. We received him with tears of entreaty in our eyes.

He took a look at Percy and nodded sagely. He knew, it appeared, all about these press-studs. He applied some olive-oil on a feather to the relevant joints, tapped twice with his pince-nez and Presto: Percy was free. It seemed almost too good to be true—all that silence. A united sigh went up from us all—a sigh such as I have never heard from dips before or since. Silence at last descended on us, the silence of a normal embassy oozing along at the normal cruising speed. No longer the goods' yards at Swindon, no longer a branch of Bassett-Lowke, no longer a boiler-makers' jamboree in Sheffield. No. Just H.M. Embassy as ever was, as ever would be in future, we hoped. But just to make assurance doubly sure Polk-Mowbray had the arms taken off the suit of armour and sent home. I can't say it improved the appearance of "The White Knight"; but then it was questionable whether anything ever could.

The Swami's Secret

I told you (said Antrobus) about the Naval Attaché and his definite leanings towards the occult? I thought I had. I don't think, however, that I ever told you about the business of the Swami. Well, the whole of my first winter old Butch Benbow, as he was laughingly called, was working away like hell on reincarnation. Breathing exercises in this office, squinting at the tip of his tongue for hours at a time until his P.A. nearly went out of her mind. He even took to holding his breath during the duller staff conferences and letting it out with a swish. This wasn't reassuring. His valet said that during the lunch interval he often sat cross-legged on the lawn with a begonia on his navel, frankly and openly meditating—but this may have been an exaggeration. Anyway, he had it bad, and he was nothing if not dogged. Indeed doggedness was clearly marked in his horoscope, he said. There was no mention of drunkenness or indecent exposure. Just the doggedness. Mind you, I myself doubted the wisdom of all this spiritual strain upon a nature which, I thought, was of a more spirituous cast, but . . . I held my peace. Even when he sprained a rib I said nothing.

Then one morning he came into my office and I was staggered by the change in his appearance. He walked like an aged and broken man. He was ashen pale. At first I put this down to the fact that we had all dined at the Burmese Legation the night before where they had served venison so rare as almost to lift one off the ground. But I was wrong. "Antrobus," he said, "I'm ruined, old man. Dished. My blasted swami is coming out by air."

"Your swami?" I echoed. He nodded and gulped.

"I've been taking reincarnation lessons by post from an Indian swami. Up to now he's simply been a Box Number in the Edgware Road, old man. Name of Anaconda Veranda. And jolly fruitful it's been up to now. But I wasn't prepared for a telegram saying that he was coming out to visit me and study my spiritual progress at first hand. He is arriving this afternoon."

"Well what's wrong with that?" I said, looking for the Silver Lining. "I bet you are the first dip. to have a private swami. Everyone will be mad with envy in the Corps." He groaned and moved from side to side, as if he were representing Colic in a charade. He said:

"My dear chap, surely you know that all swamis are little naked men in spectacles walking around with a goat on a string? What could I do with him here? I couldn't take him to cocktails with the French. I should become the laughing-stock of the whole Corps if I were seen bowling about attached to a man in a loin-cloth. The press would certainly get hold of it. What would the Admiralty say if they saw a picture of me in the Navy Weekly? You know how materialistic they are. It would mean the China Station again, and my liver wouldn't stand it."

74

THE SWAMI'S SECRET

I took a deep breath. I began to see his point. A loin-cloth is a tricky thing in diplomacy; in the hands of the Ill-Disposed it could become a Secret Weapon. I pondered.

"Well," I said at last, "you will have to try and Carry It Off somehow. Pretend he's a cousin of somebody important like Noel Coward or Bruce Lockhart. It's the only chance." But he was sunk in gloom and hardly heeded me. "And then there's another thing," he said gloomily. "I'm supposed to be living on goat's milk—not un-sweetened condensed touched up with Gordon's Dry. Somehow I couldn't bring myself to keep a goat in the house. They smell so. I expect he'll give me a dressing down on spiritual grounds when he finds out. And honestly, Antrobus, I don't see myself passing him off as a relation, do you?" To be honest I didn't really; but what was to be done? The plane had already left London with Butch's little spiritual adviser aboard. We would have to face up to reality. I confess my heart ached for old Butch.

But if he was pale now, my colleague, he was a great deal paler that afternoon as he got into the official car and set off for the airport to meet his swami. I didn't blame him. The dew of death had settled on his somewhat re-ceding brow. The poor chap could see himself socially dished as well spiritually pooped.

Imagine his relief, however, when out of the aircraft stepped—not a naked Dravidian leading a quarantined goat—but the most poised and charming of Indian princelings, clad in beautifully cut clothes and wearing a turban with an emerald the size of a goitre in it. Anaconda Veranda was perfectly delightful, a Man Of The World, a Gentleman. Butch nearly fainted with relief as he

75

listened to his perfect English, his exquisite English—rather better than Butch's own brand of the stuff. Could this be the swami he so much dreaded? Butch swooned back in his car muttering prayers of thanksgiving. By the time he reached the Embassy with his swami he was a changed man. He was swollen with pride, gloating almost.

I must say I found Veranda—everyone found him—perfectly delightful. It seems that he had been at Oxford with all of us—though strangely enough nobody remembered him. But he was as unbashfully Balliol as it is possible to be. And far from receiving the acid drop Butch found himself the most sought-after man in the Corps. All because of his swami. Veranda danced beautifully, was modest, wise, witty and gentle; he also played the flute to distraction which endeared him frightfully to Polk-Mowbray. He was even spiritually accommodating and let Butch know that in certain stages of spiritual development the odd touch of gin in unsweetened condensed is just the job and has the unofficial approval of the Dalai Lama. Butch was in ecstasies. So were we all.

Veranda did quite a bit of drawing-room occultism, turning tables and telling fortunes until the Ladies of the Corps were almost mad with flattery and apprehension. He hypnotized Drage and took an endless succession of hard-boiled eggs out of his nose. He predicted Collin's appointment to China. He told Dovebasket the size of his overdraft to two places of decimals. My dear chap, he was a Man of Parts. In next to no time he had most of the Ambassadresses pleading openly for spiritual instruction while the Heads Of Mission, mad with envy, were cabling their head office for swamis to be sent out on approval by air freight. Polk-Mowbray even conceived the idea of creating a special post of Senior Spiritual Adviser to the

Embassy and appointing Veranda to it. Just to keep him with us. But I think the Chaplain intervened and quashed the idea. Polk-Mowbray sulked a good deal after this.

Well, for a whole season Veranda occupied the social spotlight, to our intense pride. He dined here, he dined there. He was put up for the O.B.E. and the Croix De Guerre—and quite a lot of other decorations. As a social draw he was unequalled, a human magnet. And of course Butch went up to the top of the class. He had to engage a private secretary to keep his now bulging Engagements Book and head off mere climbers with the Retort Civil (but Cutting). He was a happy man.

But now comes the *dénouement*—which poor Polk-Mowbray probably refers to as "the pay-off" nowadays. It happened quite suddenly and gracefully. I must say that Veranda must have made a close social study of the Corps and its movements. He chose one of those ghastly holidays—was it Labour Day?—when he could be sure that the whole Corps was sitting on a dais in the main square of the town, perspiring freely and watching the infantry defile—if that is the word. Yes, it was beautifully conceived, perfectly timed. He started by borrowing the official car and a dozen of De Mandeville's pigskin suitcases. In leisurely fashion, and with that irresistibly endearing smile which had won so many friends and influenced so many people—he made a tour of the Embassies cleaning them out with judgement and discretion. Such selectivity, old man. Only the best seemed to be good enough. Just the top jewellery like Polk-Mowbray's dress studs, Angela's tiara . . . the top treasures like the original Leonardo drawings in the Argentine Legation, the two Tiepolos *chez* the Italians, the first edition of Hamlet in Spalding's library, the two Mycenaean brooches of the Greek Ambassadress. He even took Nelson's Dress Sword which was Butch's only real treasure and on which he always made toast in the winter. And with all this stuff safely stowed in his saddle-bags the fellow evaporated, snuffed himself out, dematerialized. . . . Well, old boy, you can imagine the rumpus. What an eruption! At first one hardly believed it. Surprised! You could have sluiced us down with frangipani. Many was the hanging head, many the pallid glance. Poor Butch found himself at the bottom of the form again—so did we all. For this terrible house-guest had become firmly identified with our Mission. I don't know how we lived through the next few months. Butch's swami was never traced, nor was any single item from all this cultural boodle. Somewhere among the bazaars of India these treasures must be on sale. One blenches to think of it.

It took Butch years to live down his swami. But the worst of it all was that he never finished his reincarnation course; somehow he hadn't the heart to go on. Nor has he ever had the heart or the social courage to try another swami. And as he hasn't mastered the drill he lives—so I understand from common friends—in perpetual terror of being reincarnated as a soldier.

9

A Smircher Smirched

It was at the corner of one of those little streets just off Piccadilly that we crashed into each other by the purest accident and flew apart. "Antrobus!" I exclaimed in surprise, and indeed with considerable concern. "Antrobus —*you running*? I would never have believed it." Yet he had been running quite hard with his hat held on by hand, his coat-tails flying. I wondered what they would say to this up at the Office. "Quick," he panted. "No time to explain. Follow me," and took off once more like a peppered hare. I caught him at the next corner where he had the grace to wait and we started walking very fast indeed. He kept glancing over his shoulder nervously. "I have just committed a Felony," he said at last. "A real one." When he made sure that we were not being pursued he drew breath and settled into his normal ambling stride, though he was still somewhat winded. "It came over me in a flash, old man. I felt the sky darken round me when I saw him. I was powerless to control my lower impulses. Just the sight of that blasted Toby Imhof, just the sight

81

of him . . . and I sloughed the upbringing of a lifetime.
But I was right. You will agree, I am sure."

"Imhof," I cried. "Not my favourite Press Officer?"

Antrobus snarled and beat the air. Between clenched
teeth he said: "The very same. Tobias Imhof Esquire,
late of H.M. Foreign Service, now Supreme Director of
Inspirational Advertising. If you had seen him as I did,
stepping out of his mother-of-pearl inlaid Rolls Royce
with red satin upholstery. . . . Dressed, old man, in a
Magdalen blazer *and* a straw boater with the Roedean
colours *and* a Rifle Brigade scarf. . . . By heavens, you
would have done as I did. The car had fake Imhof arms on
it, too, with a sort of device: a loofah with ringworm
gules with reversed nylons. I shook with rage as I saw
him lounge into the Ritz and remembered all that I had
suffered from him."

"You are rather hard on Toby," I said. "After all, he
lent some colour to the service if nothing else. Maybe he
wasn't *quite* suited for the higher diplomacy. . . ."

"Nothing became him like his leaving of it," said
Antrobus tartly. "But that is not the point. The savage
blow I struck this afternoon had nothing to do with that.
I did it on behalf of decent folk everywhere. Toby with
his infernal advertising has been within an ace of smirching *The Times* these last months. *The Times*, old cat's paw,
The Times! I tell you that top people everywhere have
been teetering, practically titubating. You yourself have
doubtless been among them, a silent witness, wondering
whether a switch to the *Telegraph* wasn't all that was left."

"I've been abroad."

"Ah! That is why. Then I owe you some explanation of
my conduct. It had nothing to do with the fake arms
either: a lot of people grew fake armorial bearings in

Vulgaria I remember. The De Mandeville escutcheon, if I am not mistaken, bore a couple of plants reclining gules on a sable background with the legend *Experimentia Docet*. His chauffeur who was private school maintained that this meant 'Asparagus Conquers All'. But no. The case of Toby was darker. He had become a National Danger. Listen, I don't have to tell you what *The Times* means to us all, and most particularly to us poor chaps up in the Office, grinding along day by day, Broken on the Wheel? Of course I don't. When you get off the bus on a winter morning feeling the nip in the air and hurry towards the office you know it will be there, waiting for you. You get your keys. You ascend. There it lies, neatly folded on your desk. You settle yourself, having taken off your goloshes, and unfold it, warming your toes the while at the gas-fire. At once you feel the ordered familiarity of things seeping into you. That vital quarter of an hour before you address your papers is worth a rest cure in itself, just you and *The Times*, alone there. Softly tiptoeing through the Personals as you tone up the cortex: reassuring yourself that the solar system is still right side up, so to speak! I trust I don't exaggerate."

"Of Course Not."

"There they all are, old and tried companions, remaining unchanged in a changing world. Little Gem Mouflet, for instance, dancing away every day in private, ready to give one confidence. Dear little Gem, how does she do it? I have often meant to drop in and ask her to teach me the Conga, but somehow never found the time. Then those Americans advertising madly for rhinoceros horns and renovated harmoniums (authentic). Then those neat exchanges of Bible quotations and code messages. 'Meet you under the clock at Victoria, Pip. Bring it with you.'

Bring what? One wonders. Often I have had a mind to turn up at Victoria out of curiosity just to see what Pip would bring, but somehow one is too rushed. Then further down one comes upon the religious zealots predicting the end of the world or inviting you to buy unvivisected mink, or inveighing against alcohol. They seem against everything delicious—though they are right about mink. But who keeps cutting up mink anyhow? They must keep it pretty dark. It should sound sinister but somehow in *The Times* nothing does; even those dark invitations to colonic lavage in South Ken, which would alert the *Sureté Nationale* in a twinkling are somehow simply beguiling. One simply thanks God that they are not compulsory in the Service and passes quietly on. They all seem to be part of the Great Scheme."

Antrobus paused reflectively for a long moment before continuing in a lower and grimmer tone: "Into this essentially ordered and rational scheme came Toby, with no refinement, no feelings for other people—particularly Top People. In he burst with his dreadful half-page advertisements for all the filthy things he was patenting. Retch, the wonder baby-syrup was the first: 'DOES YOUR BABY SOUND LIKE A WIND-TUNNEL? LET SCIENCE HELP YOU WITH RETCH.' At first it was only once a month or so, though this was bad enough. But I used to take the *Telegraph* on that day. My secretary always warned me in time. But gradually the pressure increased. Toby's horrid brain children multiplied: IN A NUCLEAR AGE YOU CAN AVOID FALL OUT ONLY WITH AN IMHOF PRAM. Figure to yourself our faces. Then came Sludge, the marvel among detergents. I grew to dread those huge diagrams of blocked drains. But that was not all. It grew worse. Toby scaled heights of horror undreamed of before. If I remember rightly it was Clog's turn next. It was, apparently, the only full cream perm, so smooth so delicious. With starting eyeballs we gazed upon the picture which illustrated it. A crêpe neck with everything but the marks of the noose on it. It turned the stomach old man. And since then it has gone on getting worse. I will pass over Scratcho, the only toilet paper in the world, as being beneath contempt. But I have only to mention Gorge, Drool and Burp to give you an idea of what has been happening down at Blackfriars. I see you have gone quite white. Yes, well you may. You can see now what has been happening. Why this very week came a series of ghastly scents for which The Moulder Of Minds had invented names like Armpit, Malentendu, and Piston-Slap. You can imagine the effect on the Office. I tell you we have all got circles under our prose."

He paused panting. It was indeed a terrible indictment of our late colleague. "But this Felony, Antrobus," I said at last. "What form did it take. Did you assault him?" Antrobus shook his head. His eyes gleamed. "Better than that. I struck a real blow at the smircher. Mark my words, it will be at least a tenner or a fortnight for being stuck outside the Ritz. I tell you, the sky simply went black around me. My action was pure and unpremeditated. Part of the road was up and there was a pile of those metal studs they put down at crossings. You know the kind? Sharp steel ends. There was also a navvy's mallet lying nearby. It was the work of a minute to drive the studs home into the cringing rubber of Toby's filthy tyres. He was still inside swilling Benedictine and gin I suppose. But by God when he comes out with those dragoman's moustaches there will be a policeman waiting for him. Mark my words."

"You punctured him, just like that, in cold blood?"

"Utterly. In all four wheels."

"Bravo, Antrobus. The Office will be proud of you."

Antrobus blushed self-deprecatingly and coughed behind his hand. "I say, you really think so?"

"I most certainly do."

"I'm awfully glad to hear it. It's my first Real Felony, you know, and I was in two minds about keeping it dark."

An idea had suddenly struck me. "I tell you what," I said. "Let's get a cab and drive up and down outside the Ritz to watch Toby get progged. Shall we?" Antrobus' face lit up with a fitful and hesitant smile. "Could we do it without being seen?"

"Of course. I wouldn't miss this for worlds. Come on."

He was still somewhat reluctant but I dragged him to a taxi and we set off. It was all just as he had said it would be. "Such joy is seldom granted us," muttered Antrobus as we crouched on the floor of the taxi, hats over our faces, drinking in the beautiful scene which was being enacted outside the Ritz. Such a crowd, too. There was Toby perspiring and swearing and fanning himself with his boater. There was the mother-of-pearl Rolls kneeling down like a camel. There was a large, a deliciously large policeman, obviously in perfect health, making notes in a book and repeating with an air of disbelief the fatal words: "O you *was* was you?" leaving little doubt that this time the smircher had been well and truly smirched.

"So scrumptious, such bliss," said Antrobus. He closed his eyes and his lips moved in silent thanksgiving for a moment. It was indeed a sigh to hearten one. We both felt the better for it, indeed positively inspired. Involuntarily we started singing (but very softly, lest the cabman hear us) the opening verses of the Foreign Service

A SMIRCHER SMIRCHED

Anthem whose words are by the immortal Harry Graham.

We were playing golf
The Day the Germans landed.
All our troops had run away,
All our ships were stranded,
And the thought of England's shame
Nearly put us off our game.